MEN UNLIKE OTHERS

JOHNNY FRANCIS WOLF

A Wild Ink Publishing Original
Wild Ink Publishing
wild-ink-publishing.com

ISBN: (Hardcover) 978-1-958531-09-9
ISBN: (Paperback) 978-1-958531-08-2
ISBN: (eBook) 978-1-958531-20-4

We should become acquainted, so pour yourself a cup of tea, wrap yourself in a blanket, and let's have a chat.

When I started my journey as a publisher, I was terrified. Sure, I was prepared in theory. I had just finished years of schooling which would bring me to this moment. This had always been my dream, but I was terrified, shivering, and green behind my ears. But I did it, I approached Johnny Francis Wolf, a poet I had been admiring from afar.

It was written in the stars. Thinking there was no way he would even consider my small company, one day I found him online lamenting over the query process of finding an agent and a publisher, and I had a moment of audacity. I commented, "Hey, I just started a publishing company and I love your work." And he took a chance on me. The stars smiled upon me.

In early conversations, it was noted that his style, his tone, his embodiment reminded us, at Wild Ink, of Freddie Mercury. We let him know that we believed this collection of poetry was his "Bohemian Rhapsody." We knew this manuscript was THAT important, that groundbreaking. Johnny slashes cookie-cutter poetry to pieces and creates his own style, his own opera. His own magnum opus, and a deep one at that. It is worthy of your time and attention.

Working with him there have been ups and downs. We have struggled to understand each other, then moments where we've understood each other so clearly that it shocked both of us. Our creative minds wrestled, argued, and created. Through it all, my time with Johnny Francis Wolf has been exhilarating. I have learned more than I have in my entire lifetime. He taught me about poetry and the passion that goes into picking every single word. He taught me the importance of each comma and every single extra space. He taught me the art and beauty of each singular word. At times he even taught me to stand up for myself, while other times, showed me how to have compassion in the face of perceived evil. I am thankful to have had this past year. Working with him has been nothing short of extraordinary.

I present to you, *Men Unlike Others* by Johnny Francis Wolf. You are about to embark on a journey that is nothing less than brilliant. He is the sort of poet people will be speaking of for millennia to come (no, that is not hyperbole). When you read this, savor every word, every piece of punctuation, and every stanza break, because each one was chosen for its artistry and impact.

Thank you for taking this journey with us. Each one of you brings your own life story to the reading of this, therefore you are taking part in the creative process that Johnny has made his life's work. My wish for you is that you enjoy, ponder, and grow.

With my gratitude,

Abigail Wild,
Wild Ink Publishing

Turnstile with Ian Tan the Editor

Friends and readers,

Ever people-watched? Not stalking. No, not at all. I'm talking about slowing down for that one rare moment in a day, taking in the mob making up your background, surrounded by folks every which way, alone in this bubble of hyperawareness.

I'm talking about that moment when you gaze up from your phone, magazine, or ham sandwich and really take it all in.

Skin, tongue, and creed are on either side, to-and-fro, on the street, or part of your commute. Society in all its cosmopoly-this-and-thatness. You'll maybe note things that sparkle. Taking in a tattoo here, a minted brand or label there. The stiffness in a stranger's stance, eyes that vex and otherwise burn, a simple rainbow bracelet. You are learning bits and pieces of your temporary travel-mates if only for a fleeting moment before they must move on.

Early in our journeying, I asked Johnny if there were themes and patterns besides the obvious and orderly alphabetical. I wanted a little heads-up to make collective sense of the pieces I was about to edit. He wrote:

"I initially assembled my manuscript imagining it akin to a NYC subway car... a slew of unrelated faces sitting across the train aisle, every one of them fascinating in their own unlikeness. Our gaze moving from one to the other.

Each sees the world singularly. Disparate pasts, hopes, and dreams. Yet all wondering what to have for lunch. This way different, and related.

As with the 160 stories and poems I present in alphabetical order, there's no planning who sits next to whom. These are faces on a train. My train."

———

Friends, I have no way of prepping you for every individual poem or story. But if you can see this as a people-watching opportunity, observing signs and shapes, eavesdropping on lovers cooing, peeking into someone life or gated window minus drapes, then you will find the sheer brilliance that gave me chills while reading.

The question is, will this give you what you need to interpret all you witness? No, surely not. The Chinese dialects of Cantonese, Mandarin, Hokkien et al. might hold little distinction to a non-speaker's ear, but know they are distinctly different. Similarly, not likely every queer reads the same. Heroes can be darker, layered. Losers sometimes win.

Commuters hold their secrets close.

In that same way, some of you may grapple with the elaborate vocabulary. Others might, at first, find the stylistic format patterning much of Johnny Francis Wolf's storytelling unfamiliar. Still, some may experience shock when given entry into a culture so different from their own. Our author's trek has taken him to many places, in dreams and tangible reality. In this journey expect to go down tracks less traveled. The book is titled *Men Unlike Others* for a reason. You must know that you are not taking this strange, new ride alone. As Johnny's first privileged fare, I've learned a lot about him, myself, and about Life.

I'm on the train with you.

———

If you are fresh to the poetry scene, there are pieces throughout that are shorter, simpler, even warm, wacky and pleasurable. Take your time coasting through the book, maybe flip ahead, if you like, to find these lighter palate cleansers waiting to invite you within. As for the more ornate and tangled pieces, those that mire quickened strides, they beg to be taken nice and slow. Allow yourself sink in, let them seep into your soul. Don't push yourself to understand all the sundry odds and ends, even if prone to solving, cracking cryptic mysteries.

Allow the ride, the prose, the verse to whelm you with rhyme and pattered words like the sound of a train on olden tracks.

Friends, I urge you linger, to murmur lines out loud as reading (all the better to hear flow and rhythm), to explore new words and worlds if they pluck your curiosity. You could ride a subway till you're grey and never really *know* your train-mates. And maybe that's okay. Perchance you might see them on your next commute and spot something fresh to appreciate and savor.

Sit still, stay open while the subway hurtles through a darkened tunnel, one lit station to the next; you *will* arrive at somewhere new. But come, come, I've rambled on enough...

You there, Sir, might I ask the time? *11:30 am?* Wonderful, train's ready and waiting. Enjoy the ride.

And you, young miss, what time must you be on your way? *3pm?* Well, right on schedule, pass on through.

Lads, careful over there, *don't jostle.* Yes, I heard the same as you, that Santa might be found aboard, keep an eye out.

Animals? *Ah... well, of course.* Do show some love if spot a dog near someone's knee or drooling cat on lap.

Our next stop is 14th Street and Union Square.
Stand clear of the closing doors, please.

Title of the book refers to the author's typic connection with no one.   At least to few.

A voluntary sequester..   deeming to be different by design.

Whilst *sensitive*, *gay*, and *brooding* is not an unusual trio of descriptors — required reading for some Creatives — *his* particular combination of these and other manners more unruly makes for a lot of not fitting in.

He details some of this factious flummery here, relating it all to his tilt toward **men**, love of **animals**, fondness for **writing** — a disparate coterie of sundry druthers for some — interwreathed and inextricably tangled for him.

Whether with words veiled or self–evident, pithy else limerical, honeyed vs. grim, real ere imagined — Johnny writes of and for humans like himself..

   ... and men unlike others.

dédié à

girl named Wolf and boy called Fran
both bouquet his nom de guerre

lavender of mingled ink.

fragrant always
ever there.

A thru **C**

C thru F

F thru I

I thru L

A thru C

From childhood's hour I have not been
As others were — I have not seen
As others saw — I could not bring
My passions from a common spring —

From the same source I have not taken
My sorrow — I could not awaken
My heart to joy at the same tone —
And all I lov'd — I lov'd alone —

ALONE

– Edgar Allan Poe

afternoon

—

R esisting that which should be done,
 I settled 'pon the couch.

Scanned a tome, a thinly one..
 reposed within a slouch.

—

Fervor rising, doffed my shirt,
 the pictures stirred ado.

Further stretched, my feet inert
 save curling toes, askew.

—

—

Heat of day took over sense
　　of apropos and apt..

What I read, in its defense,
　　had seized and kept me rapt.

—

Suddenly the comfy chair
　　bore flesh bereft attire,

and all I planned to do and care
　　for left to morrow's mire.

—

—

Self–amusement took control
     and in my hand I held...

..Shall we grant my only goal
     was pleasure, much impelled.

—

Lovely was the apogee,
     flow with lots of frappe.

Afterwards, as often be..
     I took a naked nap.

—

ago

I nquired if I had a light. I turned,
beheld his eyes... Lit a match
to shine upon as smoke began to rise.

Cerulean with haloed edge, gilded
my desire... Flame and gaze 'til one
became an iris blazing fire.

Cigarette adorned his lips as orbs
were wet with sting... Fumes are never
kind to blue.. this fragile coloring.

. . . .

Drawn to corners holding tears, blushed
the humble white... Pink and blue now
blending hue.. closer look, I might..

for ever nigh I needed peer, view
the breaking stare... Borderline of
rude, I fear.. bid bold and unaware.

To taste the savor, smoky tease, tongues
betray the truth... as nicotine and flesh
affix a memory of youth.

ALABASTER
(achromic meditations)

Born too white and SMOOTH of skin,
remember Father's stare.
UNFORGIVEN, loathsome sin..
Never had a prayer.

~ ~

CREAMY DOLLOP, spoonful rot,
spilled behind the crypt.
Clearly TEMPTING splooge I shot,
a child shaking, stripped —

~ ~

Priest did slurp and swallow all,
hungry for the TASTE,
TENDER fear, the smell of small.
My youthful flesh unchaste.

LUSCIOUS how I felt as toy,
Son who would confess
to he who WHISKED and whipped his boy..
I live my life as less ——

~ ~

Fabled pearl of pallid light,
feints the hoary HOST.
Bairn is blamed, 'tis His to SMITE
for spill of seeded Ghost.

~ ~

Waxen paste of cherished wan,
vernal craved for BLOOM..
SPRING and stainless sought, this swan.
Bleached and blenched, their spume.

Peak of foam, anemic yeast..
grooming lathered squirt.
CHURCH that offers fresh as feast,
TOPPING as dessert.

~ ~

Ruination, stripling's ASH,
brushly broomed in bin.
PAY the scraps with tithing's cash
and mea culpa thin —

,

~ ~

Furry beasts and FLUFFY friends
where humans ever failed.
Odd to note the dog who mends
me — ALABASTER tailed.

alee

I'd not spent the prior evening in pursuit of grande and noble endeavors.

Was a madcap essay into getting laid.

The brasher aspects of my.. shall we say, *'procurement'*.. included several questionable wingmen, a surfeit of unsavory locales, and numerous indelicate women who played upon our generous natures as flagons were rife and emptied.

I was nothing if not the victim.

———

And there, sun rising and aiming shivs directly at my sclerae, with sand chafing certain, erm.. *'tender'* and commonly *'harbored'*.. areas of dermis, I found myself delirious and supine on a beach. Naked...

a lady's chiffon scarf wreathed securely about my wrists, my wallet open and chasmal but 3 feet to my starboard, toenails jungle red and sparkly, with disparate cards and donor id between each dactyl cleavage.. no doubt some sportive attempt at making the lacquer's application more precise and tidy...

my phallus still (oh dear).. *'boastful'*.. having a better recall of the evening than your author, seemingly.. spoke of good times and turgid opportunities when my own head was pounding.. not in that same good way.

————

Freeing my wrists, noticing my fingernails an unflatteringly dissimilar shade to my toes, I modestly positioned the diaphanous scarf (lovely patterned floral with beryl highlights) around my buttocks as I rolled over, worried in my twilight drift that it would likely take flight.

So stuffed it, I did, well into my crack to affix it.. anchored and fast.

Fact that I was overwhelmingly, as yet, undraped everywhere else, mattered less to me at that moment.

I slept.

————

I recall flashes, trices.. twinklings, if you will.. when I roused, sputtering spew, coughing up the prior evening's beverage of choice now mixed with both bile and the stale, smoke–filled rooms within which they were imbibed.

Muffled voices tried enter my dream.

"Are you alright, laddie?   Should we send for transport?"
whispered the wraiths attending my trance...

as faeries deemed lower pink and blue plaid upon my lack,
gathered wallet and trifling contents left nigh, and some bits of
clothing not taken by wind...

slipping henley and boxers under my head.. discreetly burying
barf with sand.. and tucking my sundries 'neath me and the
donated wool.

———

I was finally and fully awakened by the afternoon's light rain.
In the pearl mist that dampened the shore that early Autumn,
there were few strollers braving the soon–to–be steady pelt.

For me it felt good, like palliatives melting remnants of pain.

The fuzzies had gone.. leaving myself and dogs.. them licking
my face, before they would race to catch up with owners
expounding with fellow roaming compeers on Parliament this
and Royals are that.

———

I was suddenly and singularly happy.

A foreign conceit for me. I'd not thought much of the doctrine in years.

Had resigned to live a life of verity.. the fallacy of others' sooth.. only peppered with the occasional deviant picnic... these wanderings and junkets with friends and alone (the latter generally more satisfying) decidedly more rare of late.

And the happiness quotient involving said dalliances.. less and less with time's forward slog as skin's veneer and want doth crack.

Whilst those adjuvant (*piffle*, primary focus) of such expeditions hint evermore young, I add rumples to jaw and eye.

Today was not the same.

The salt spray left me fresher and drawn, vellum more taut.. resolved in what years managed be left.. to live more joy, whatever vestige of bloom remained.

Offer more my truth.

——

And there, in the distance, a vision of Sam...

colleague from my germinal years of keeping grosses and nets..

(though hardly did he fit the auditor's boilerplate... too swarthy and buckling ever to be unduly distracted by interests accrued).

Died in his youth, victim of things he did in the dark. Someone I knew from afar...

and close.

―――

Coming to meet me from out of the waves.. a baptism in reverse, 'twould appear.. as he and I seemed wax confused.

And just like that, again asleep.. beneath the plaid...

was not alone.

auto–not–biography

Unlikely that it didn't happen
just that way to
someone

else.

As ever claimed, was not
his tale, no vita very
treatise of his
veritas

and yet..

Felt a fusing
still–warm weld..

solder, brazing words he wrote
with those that framed
a photograph.

"Fiction... not of me,"
he'd say.

"Not at all...."

avowed.

Then why his blood was
in the ink,

mixed the molten lead that bound
the twain at hip and
heart?

Heat between

a pen and
boy..

'twixt the pages,

twining
two.

autres temps
(autres mœurs)

:

Stood there in the back of bus
but forward of the rearward wheel ——

WAITING for the tiny suite
(the one enclosed
in painted

steel)

: :

—— its door to open, VACANCY,
as if I needed use

the loo.

So much my life was pretense blended,
tended toward things
untrue.

:

:

Score was more I could not sleep —
WOULD RARELY slumber
Greyhound seat.

And he whose back of pew I leaned

was wholly unaware,
it seemed.

: :

Assuming so, as much I ooze
that I'M HALF NUTS
deportment
fuze

— but maybe buses gather those
and one who lives in
danger knows..

:

:

If not for all the ARMOR PLATE
that havens us from
other's fate,

Knights who ride the bus

— *'twas late.*

Just needed
stretch my toes.

:

baith

It was the combination.. the gentle stirring of unencumbered jumblement, unrelated in any way I could glean. Interbred colors, flowers and blotch..

I suffered them willingly — inspecting too close.

Styles posolutely not current, though I'd be hard–pressed to call them, at least specifically, retro. Fabrications and patterns that seemed, in fact, rescued from a Goodwill deposit bin..

Their debatably uneasy, undoubtedly ill–fit fettle was, yet, oddly pleasing..

iii

I was compelled to stare simply for the *fashion*, all the amalgamate bob and weave — braided and tangled, forced and fused — a draped display of lumpy merge..

...had nothing to do with the *bodies* beneath.

I'm sure.

iii

baptism

Told you not to bother me whene'er I take a bath.
Little time to tarry lone..   Please..   *do the fucking math..*

Lotta hours spent with you, cooperative I be.
Tub is mine when smoke is too..   Alloweth this for me..

~ ~

Sugar Daddy, grab me that, use it on my back.
So sorry, didn't mean to bark...   Civility, I lack.

Oooh...   you scrub it nice and hard...   like the way you stroke.
Lower please, if fall inside..   And join me in my soak..

Sure we'll fit with folded legs, arms about my waist.
Lips you work on bar below..   Soap on rope for taste.

Mmm...   you know the way I like it, suds with spray and spew.
Pass the ashtray, will you Pops?   *Swallow..* love you too..

~ ~

Shhhh...   so glad you fixed your will and left me so much stuff.
Gigolo who lets you play..   Well, seems I've had enough.

Garbled gasps and silent screams, all froth from rising bubbles,
steeped in dreams of future bright...

bereft of Daddy troubles.

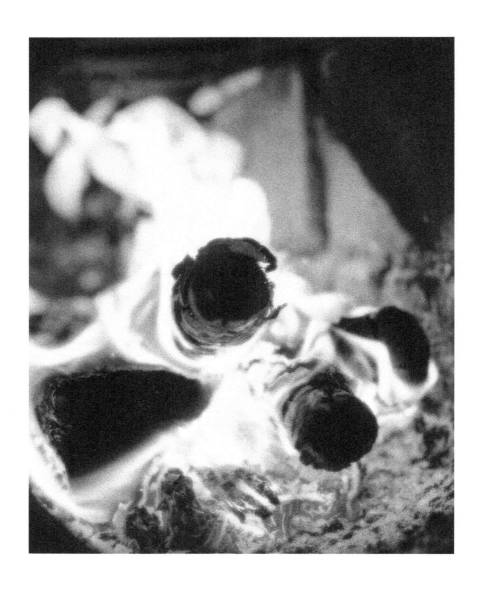

be lit

Very willing, trilling sound,
    warbled thin and fat around.
        Something added queer among
            choired angels — new their tongue.

i i

From reindeer hooves and *"Ho-Ho-Ho's"*
    to singing elves and Rudolph's nose.
        ———— The overture of doling toys,
            trolling chimneys, Christmas noise.

i i

Santa squeezing 'tween the bricks
    with blistered toes from fires' licks.
        Adding shrieks to Yuletide gay —
            flaming fur and charring sleigh.

i i

Beard no longer snowy white,
    Old St. Nick — *ablaze in flight.*
        After downing rum and nogs,
            don't forget to douse your logs.

begging pardon
(picnic prig)

L ived a nap that slipped between
my lunch and early sup,

faerie sparkled, wondrous scene...
two cats, a horse, and pup.

Meadowed thicket, grassly laid,
upon a checkered throw,

drinking wine to hazard's fade,
regarding verse of Poe.

+

His, the Raven, joined our troop
and raised a glass for toast,

*"Son, your quill doth loop–de–loop...
abests my prior host!"*

I humbly blushed as dog didst yelp,
the pussies plainly purred,

horse, of course, required help..
the wine, his whinny, slurred.

Winks and twinkles, mused upon
    the laud from ebon beak,

but all forgot when bottle gone..
    'twas doze would sooner seek.

Dream within a dream for me
    as nod within a snooze.

Smiling, woke to disagree
    with Raven, must refuse...

+

"Fair and fawning, feathered guest,
    your compliment unearned,

and yet I feel, at your behest,
    inflamed, to wit, unburned.."

Savored with a grain of salt,
    I bid them each adieu,

when gathered up the crumbs my fault
    and stardust kisses, blew.

Whiskered, maned, and she with tail
(too drunk to wag too much)

said their leavings, day now pale,
to blackbird.. *"Stay in touch."*

In blink of eye and flap of wings
I stirred from nap alone.

Sleepy hubris, ego sings...
of bluster, I am prone.

+

berg

H

ardly all they said it was.
  Underwhelming.. point of fact.

Granted, morning light, sipping Earl Grey steeped on deck —
watching riggers tighten knots and ropes.. hawsers loosened
overnight — gilded peaks of glacial cap would prism out in
compass search.. rivulets of overlap upon the frigid crystals..
perch.

Incandescent blinks and bluster edged the sails and beamed
off beams. Phosphorescent pinks would cluster, hearkened
morrow's dawning dreams.

Glowing bears, marooned upon the massive floes, seemed
blaze and gleam — from furry glints of chilly swim to hoaried
hints of bitter glim..

^ ^ ^

Borealis Eos, cracked of finely frizzled fans of flash, might dash
across and wipe the sky, as sunlight glistered lower still..

'til wrapped our schooner, sooner thrill.

  No..

.. disillusioned, as I say. Better shine midst circus tune, kaleidoscopic rainbow moon, trousselier with lantern's rune — all could make such pageant shy.

And yet these words, avowed, belie. For none of this was seen before, uncharted map to parlayed peril..

venture thinly iced.

^ ^ ^

Clipper tacked to miss the mass, appeared aslant of bow.... it sliced.

^ ^ ^

Glassing glaze, a passing maze, and with it sundered wood...

severed Mermaid's lacquered prow.. leaving us to swim, and now.

Splintered bits of sunrise ghost, aurora felt as bland as toast — as reaching out to wrap our arms around a floating sailor's swell, whose rigoured face be facing down — did not dissuade my languor well.

Boring as a Sunday nap, and equally embraced.
Sliding, sinking 'neath its lap...

my lethargy, at last, replaced.

^ ^ ^

blur
(when we marched)

Déjà vu of Future me

        is not yet then, but there I be.

Hazy clouds, I REMINISCE

        the coming times, a Past I miss.

= = =

Here I am with latter you,

        an older self but FLEXING NEW..

Shadow people shunning light,

        fuzzy shapes invade my sight.

WHERE I AM is nowhere now
　　　　and why was when and who is how.

Only know I'll not return
　　　　to what I'm leaving.. left to burn.

= = =

Vagaries seem amply norm
　　　　as whims and fancies round me, swarm.

Foggy id to ego skewed..
　　　　for NEBULOUS my only mood.

Maybe this is for the best,
          my heart still beating, FEELING BLEST.

Forward thinking, far and soon
          whilst facing Sun, reflecting Moon..

= = =

CLARITY IS OVERRATED..
          muddled thoughts, I'm inundated.

Floating with the other Souls
          when in and out the open holes.

boots

Loosened laces, easy on..
my morning chores and marathon.

Witnessed not them getting old
when never had them once resoled.

. .

Facing forward, near the door,
them blending with the wooden floor.

Norman Rockwell blunted stare
as eyes who peer through muck and wear.

. .

Were they always brown and bent,
these bought or borrowed, stolen, lent..

if ever were they boxed and new
or birthed an old and wizened shoe ?

but maybe an Angel

"I give Him what He needs,
not asks."

I paraphrase from some
apocalyptic film
I liked.. from not that
many years ago.

An Angel speaketh of the Lord
as if He were not perfect,

as if He needed someone there
to tell Him, *"Hey —*

You're naked."

What if 'perfect' simply
means it's RIGHT, right now,
but only at that
very time..

Can shift when something,
someone happens,

switches things and varies
view, mitigates.

Like you.

Like when we pray,
"Hey Dude.   How could you
let that awful thing,

that thing that killed that
Baby Boy...

How could you let that pass?"

So maybe, then, He might well say,
"You know...   I never
thought like
that.."

And mend His ways and
bring the Child,

bring him
back to
Life.

An Angel such as
you or me
can
maybe

change His mind.

by now
(backseat)

What started out a boyhood crush led to Forest Park —
back of Dodge with pleather plush — the vinyl scribed its mark.

    Lattice work on derriere, the safety belt and clamp —
    etchings left, no longer there — the sticky stuck with damp.

. . .

Such was all I had to show for all that sweat and slop —
all the carnal mop and glo — and all the spit we'd swap.

    Little am I keen educe, as much I craved it then —
    except for bids bereft of juice — the start.. I'd live again.

First began before we climbed from front to back of coupe —
grazing lips, afore were slimed — and flesh was not yet soup.

There, the crux of all I ask, if all I queried real —
essence, pith, and paring masque — the KISS is all we feel.

. . .

Rest is rather 'side the point, peripheral to plot —
moment hallowed, deemed anoint — devoid of all that snot.

For messy is the fun of youth, but older what we seek —
is someone to remember truth —

was you, and not your leak.

canis lupus

Bestride the river, morning quo,
sun through lens and squared its glow..

      with feral bend to ancient throat,
      frosted mist from pelaged coat.

If rising brume be borne of howl..
mingles pyre, hunt and prowl.

i i i

      Rapture lifted Goshen heights,
      their capture gifted, feastly nights.

Blessings sung and fossils praised,
an invitation..   bygones razed..

      Dwell, endure, persist, *prevail*.
      Isle of Man and primal Gael.

Hoary weald enshrouding copse
as o'er the wail the scrimmage stops.

> Joust and brawl and warfare lay
> below the clouds that steam from brae.

Looms the wraith that mizzles murk,
is soaring over loch and cirque.

iii

> Brute that flies bereft of wing
> and lords above, on four, this King..

Coterie beneath his guard,
aegis shelter, fortress scarred.

> Halberd spear to fiend divine
> where safe abaft and postern line.

Soldier, Satan, Seraphim,
stalker, scoundrel.. bloodied limb..

       crying shrill and screeching shriek,
       keening sorrow, moments weak.

O, such creature, savage trope
as one couldst quill and author hope..

             i i i

       Augustly oded, ogred rake,
       thirst to quench and carnal, slake.

Not of this nor any Earth.
Not a beast begot in birth.

       Likely not the Wolf you deem
       but prima facie *id*, wouldst seem...

can't

Burning, never turning, toward his chin and skin that smell of smoke — in SWEAT and limber, timber spruce — will axe an afternoon —

with denim slung about his hips, too loose for all those TWISTS and shouts — as cleaving wood and cracking bole, to crash to earth too soon.

NOR will ever kiss those lips that beg for wet in midday glare — who laugh when hose I hold doth SPLASH across a tender face —

where glistened torso 'gainst the tree, of lean and leg when in between — he sings me of a morning breeze and all I hear is GRACE.

—

Mingle not his flesh with mine, for raised my family ever
high — above the one with WHISKERS close, and whispers
in my ear —

a SIMPLE boy with nary not, and cannot give me what I
want — though what I want is endless holding him alone,
is clear.

WILL NOT yield, am sure of it, so firm I will not FEEL what
tugs my — heart and jeans — of no appeal — nor notice
when they fall —

—

there he'll stand and, likewise too, be SKIN and searching,
like we do — when humans love and yet with adze —
will HEW and hack our all.

—

caught on film

Perilous, the stakes were high.   Would not yield nor sanctify the status quo presented with.. the mark he'd earned, the man, the myth.

Fedora's tilt was not, in fact, a part of who he was, unpacked.   Was simply sloped for better fit.. when face to face, encountered *'it'*.

And sneer that gird his face with flout, which peered through blackened eyes, throughout.   Not a show of force or spite.. but rather more a tender bite.

ii

Inviting he who feigned alone, who likewise knew his cover blown.. resist the urge to pivot, run. Wouldst sooner bid this one on one.

And I who heard the sound of night, in alley dark with want of light.. didst flash my lens upon the pair who stood together, spooning there.

Years of fleeting twists of fate, loathing self, for others, hate.   Dyad turning, lips aflame.. cheeks on fire, me to blame.

charity

A fair amount.. more than that,
but less than most would think —

> Helium, you buoyant grip
> who reared a bloated, bladdered ship

— when thought atop.. would sink.

* *

Patched with surplus scraps and shreds
of others, meting me —

> Pleasings offered, measured, doled,
> indebtedness of mine, controlled

— expected on my knee.

Grovel, blandish, charm, caress
their hand and all they ply —

        Kiss what bid these gifts upend..
        fixing boy they loudly mend

— or else *'ungrateful'* cry.

* *

As if within a black and white
bygone film of erst —

        Stewart spouting Capra's creed,
        and I am not a goodly lead

— but actor likely cursed.

For no one helps without a toll,
assistance carries score —

       and we who only wish a meal,
       job to work and pillow feel

— made less for wanting more.

           * *

Ahh, yes, unloose your rolling eyes
above the us below —

       *"All you monkeys living free,
       the same you echo.. 'Pity me.'*

— *Thankless shit you throw !"*

Charlie—in—the—Box

ONCE UPON A TIME
THERE LIVED..

an odd little whore named Charlie —

Who.. 'twas said (I can't help grin)..
thought himself... *a masseur.*

— — —

But most who knew him, and all who purchased his of–an–ilk ministrations, understood just what he was quite well.   The only confused one was he.

Not that Johnny (of course I mean Charlie) wasn't driven by the noblest of intent... especially true when first pursuing his apical craft.   But quickly discerned folks were far more munificent, giving of alms and donations, when massages were more, um — *tangled.*

(Though Charlie loved women, were men who mostly sought such release.)

— — —

Attractively built, tall and athletic,
strong jaw..   not small in the 'talent' department...

Charlie, naïve, owned little of this. His life outside his humble abode, most often robed chaste... simple and seemly, covered up good.. hiding all skin and bone —

sharpened the contrast when working with patrons, completely exposed.... indeed fully nude.

———

Filled to the brim with fears, insecurities. Chockablock, unrealized dreams.

An actor, too scared. A writer, not writing. An artist, no canvas.

Believer, but no Church would have him.

But *this* he could do.

———

Intuitive hands, compassionate heart, hurt not his business.. as much as the obvious kept men returning.

But unlike his peers, fellow Hollywood hustlers, he comforted all, nihil denied — victims of stroke, vets without limbs, cancer survivors, colostomy bagged, obese, misshapen, quadriplegic, elderly, frail, paralyzed, Aids.

Looking for love, they found the right place.

And yes, there were pretty ones.   Treated the same.
(We're ALL only steps 'way from lame.)

— — —

He lived in the Land of Misfit Toys, *thrilled* to bring
dwellers his measure of joy.   Felt blessed could
'perform' with any and whole..

a gift he was given, by God (or whomever), to please
and be pleased, heal and be healed..

Untouchables touched (and he by default).

— — —

But those wracked with guilt, the curious/straight,
were ever the hardest to slake.   Deformities hid, pain
lying beneath, no curative stroke of a palm could reach.

From giddy beginnings to making–love middles, lasting
through (un)happy endings — then dressed, money
cast, ran from his hearth — headed for wives, children,
home.

Safe haven he gifted was now but reviled.   And well
if they could...

wouldst kill the messenger (missive too dear)..
their only lust left...   he took care of the rest.

Delivered that pell with merely a touch, wordlessly
reading from scroll — as verity bare — already they
knew — for deeply extant within.

There, at his feet, would lay when they entered. Thence,
would they leave with it laden on back.

Even debriefings, for just such occasions...
    revulsion, repulsion, repugnance repaid.

            They'd call to return, but a month to the day.

——— ——— ———

Helped who he could, letting go of the lost.   Lived in
his box (no 'popping' with song) his eyes to the
ground when venturing topside, knowing his place
in the World.

Knew from the lessons he learned on the Altar —

Toys such as he, were destined for Hell.
Priests taught him well.
                                    (Ironic, true that.)

——— ——— ———

Prayers and love for Charlie and Mary (the harlot who bathed Jesus' feet).

Choirs of Angels are with you tonight...

and maybe 'tis Angels you be.

— — —

C thru F

Those who have never known a lover's sin
Let them not read my ditty, it will be
To their dull ears so musicless and thin
That they will have no joy of it, but ye

To whose wan cheeks now creeps the lingering smile,
Ye who have learned who Eros is — O listen yet a—while.

CHARMIDES

– Oscar Wilde

chattel
(idée fixe)

Vassal serving needs of who,
as liege men will
provide,

deeming douse the flames divined
when steeping me
inside.

" " "

Awaits with head of stoop and bow
and torso tucked in
crook..

obeisance knelt, salaaming praise,
his homage suffered
brook.

Vendible commodity,
asset line of
goods..

amenity of thrash and thrill,
relieving morning
woods.

" " "

Drudge detained and hostage held
wholly 'gainst his
will.

Master, when appointed such,
to bleed me stiff
until..

renege, rescind, our vice as void,
countermand this
game.

Slave returned to harvest glebe
as serf denuded
name.

" " "

Callous, may you slander me,
recriminate my
port..

but furlough of the carnal breed
cannot be sold too
short.

Christian in Name Only

"He gathers the LAMBS in His arms
and carries them close to His HEART..."

Isaiah 40:11

——

Anon, was to write a
snarkier verse....

CINO HYPOCRISY.

Finding this image
        displaced my thirst..

                Title remained, words did not.

——

A sated RELATE...

will pick up a cat, kneel before
dog, stand beside
horse.

I hold them, their fur
to my FACE.

We on the SPECTRUM
connect.

HE in the canvas
is CHRIST.

— —

Makes me a CHRISTIAN?
No, I don't think.

Makes me more CHRIST–LIKE?
I am unfit.

— —

Makes me AUTISTIC.
For hugging the soft of a

beast so close
        to nape and pate

                (as arms to heart)

is one of the
SIGNS..

JESUS
... *autistic*

kinda makes sense.

——

cinema, in 4 acts

[1]

Let it crumble

Wall that muffles sound and voices —
silence breathing, cede them in.

If you listen nigh to lobe, the song
between our mortared brick
seeps like light or
tiny ant

and sings of things
forgot, misplaced —

Maybe we were bundled apt,
paper wrapped with pretty bow,
moored behind the stone and slab
to never bide we
burn again.

[2]

Let it slip

Cloak of hiding wince and tremble —
level hood and suffer gaze.

Hazard slant at other's stare who
sooner bids your newborn
lamb scramble up on
hobbled limb

*to walk allayed of
cope and splint —*

Maybe semblance sewn of silk,
camouflage of masquerade,
cowers 'neath your coat, concealed.
Shields from cold but weight
too dear.

[3]

L et it tire

Arm that locks another far —
welcome weakness, muscle lax.

Would that brace be tapered 'tween,
yielding touch and reaching
sway, drawing closer
weary ghosts,

nearer yet to
cradle, fold —

Maybe strength of birr and brute
presses well and hard apart,
sinews safe from scathe and scarring.
Pray appeased, be drained
of push.

[4]

L et it be

Cannot pledge the end will bear —
any more than lone.   But life

under tweed, in clench and tomb is
living less than coma's swoon.
Billet buried, shovel
yourn.

No one wins what
no one whirls —

Dervish dancing solo still
is moving in the opened out.
Be thee entered joust and tilt...

showing up is something
(all).

clothing optional

Solid pecs like shiny mounts,
delts with ROUNDED PEAKS..

Abs, a pack of six I count,
ripe and ready cheeks.

/ /

Shoulders broad, waistline halved,
arms with biceps stout.

Firmly thighed and shapely calved,
MY APPETITE wills out.

Perfect face tops perfect vee
as nakedly he strides.

NUDIST POOL, he walks by me..
I fantasize a ride.

/ /

And what of this that dangles such,
the thing I daren't say.

Let be said the word is *'MUCH'*
..imposingly displayed.

Maybe swim a couple laps
BEHIND HIM in his lane.

Carrot/stick for me, perhaps.
Closer nigh, I gain.

/ /

Enervating, waning plash,
I'm waxing TOWARD FAINT

'til happen ogle, more a flash,
his arching bum and taint..

colorful

Perhaps I am a prism,
shades of simple mixed with gray.

Maybe I don't fit the ism..
third degree on Judgment Day.

—

"Were you always kind?"
Indeed I was, as sweet as blue.

Color of the Sky, I find
as nice as any ocean view.

—

"Did you love the Earth?"
Indeed I did, as plain as green.

Plants and trees for all their worth,
climate change to lima bean.

"Brook you fond of Beast?"
Indeed adore, as pitch as coal.

From midnight steed to tiny least,
as picnic ant to raven's soul.

—

"Couldst you ever lie?"
Indeed I can't, as true as red.

Swear to God on cherry pie,
with tree un–axed and fib un–said.

—

"Wouldst you others blame?"
Indeed I won't, as precious gold.

Even as the Sun and flame
can never really hate the cold.

"Have you doubtless sinned?"
Indeed I cede, as flawed as pink.

Like pigs that fly on wing and wind..
roses, now and then, can stink.

—

"Allow you ever killed?"
Indeed I have, as purple rain.

Grapes were crushed, wine glass filled,
unwittingly some brain cells slain.

—

"But are you not a Gay??"
Indeed I am, as rainbow flag.

Ere aspersions cast, I pray..
as why you Angels dress in drag?

Corduroy tent

: : : :

H
is words were such
he made it hard
to masque my homophilic bard.

Frankly, just a turn of phrase
delivered by his deftly laid

and finely oozing pen —

I'd cross my knees,
place tome
on lap,

to tame the
beast beneath, again.

: : : :

: : : :

He knows he wields a
mighty sword
and my own blade is his,
untoward.

Dear Lord,

Return to when
you stilled your soul,
when staid the sonnet spoke.

Go back and
quell the quill you poke —
to sleep again
the heart you woke —

: : : :

: : : :

I've nary naught elixir,
blood, nor
BVD's to trash —

Throw down not glove
per verses 'bove

— a boner begs
betwixt my
legs —

YOU WRITE NO MORE !!

E'er,
Poet Whore

: : : :

dark
(when first noted)

See but small of nape and neck
with arc of torso stooped.

Wool bedoffed and spare bedecked
as naked luring looped.

''

Framed within a youthful prank,
a memory recalled..

day you stayed the night we drank,
alighting floor..   we crawled.

Scuttled laughter, scaling bed,
endeavored not revive.

Shucked of clothes as worries shed,
asleep and yet alive.

"

Dreamt with arms and blanket shared,
shivered more as one..

when sandman left us to his lair
and neither woke with sun.

Whelmed astir as lone amid
the sheets now fleeced of form.

Curtains drawn as foreday bid
a bed bereaved of warm.

"

Laid distrait with tender ache,
tequila losing fight.

Thirsting which I could not slake
as truth of dark came light.

déjà vu

A nd when the hour bends toward two
my thoughts diverge, return to you

a wanderlust of focused fix
as lost, a stray, for food does tricks.

ˋ ˋ

— Home I find in Gypsy sleep
from scattered dreams to swaddled heap

for not alone, this swarming swerve
is loving you as spoon to curve.

ˋ ˋ

And only then to feel un—one
by vagary of wraith begun

twilight tarried trance and crave
my nightly spectre slips from grave —

desiccant

Almost like a tiny angel. Cherub maybe, feathers slight.   Wings too crisp to embers wend..

> *jejune,* her crude attempt at flight.

Juiceless veins to rainless pores... anhydrously my tongue adores.

But not when firstly happened 'pon..
> a harlot shapely, *whistling swan.*

———

Thusly was, when came of late... visage she, a pallid fate.   My overbite and humble smile bartered her what coin could guile.

Perceived her joy as buxom oozed with drizzly dew, *if dimly used.*   So much so, felt no compunction ..eased the burden on her bones which curved their bowed support of mirth...

> her earthly, ample lust of girth.

"Trust, my dear, I'll facile quell.   Will thank me."
Sank my teeth in well.   Flesh that meshed with
mouth like soup..

    borscht..   but warmly, formly..   *goop.*

Withered down to comely wench with pearl her mien
and white her blench.

———

Similitude she gleaned in glass of silver backing,
mirrored lass was so caught up with what beheld
of echoed youth and figure flattered, wanted more
was all that mattered..

"Sir, I beg you find a way to slake your thirst for
further sway..   ere you quench your sate.

For I could use a wee more lighten..

    have your fill, my beastly...   *tighten."*

Venture did I answer prayer as disappeared..   her glut
too spare..   cloying screams, as dwindled shape...

and still with lips I drew from nape.

Of nectar drank as more she shrank..
and thankly bidding swill..   *until...*

––––

Nothing left but grizzled ash that fell from neck and
décolletage. And there in hand from hence to fore,
a lovely grinning

"...tipple more."

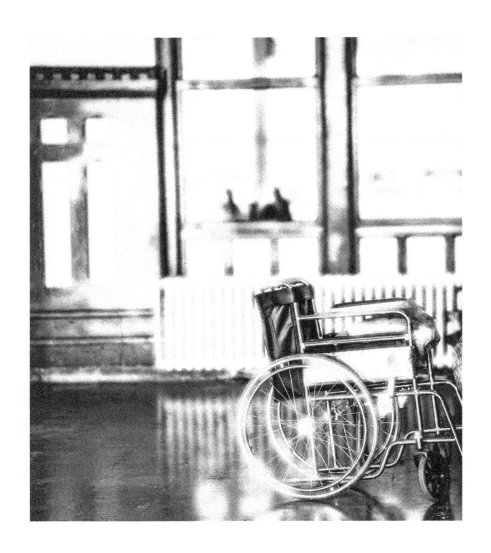

dinner

Wasn't so much I gave him a pass
or gloried the plusses

with smoke–and–mirrors
hiding the lacks
and cracks

relax..   I left out one detail

mind you and granted, a rather large
basal
encompassing cue

*"Big guy, imposing, impressive —
don't stare."*

Nothing misleading

indeed, was exemplar
with meat and potatoes arranged
on his frame, would take lots of liniment
oil him up

except that it won't.

Legs blown off, clean to the hips...

how magically managed, his dick
didst remain, spite of
the shrapnel and
stiches and
scars

spite of
the fact that everyone asks
so why I wrote it
so plain.

God has a sense of humor, I think
and gosh, he'd look great
with thighs as pumped
and round as
glutes

but no —

War is quite the artist, designer
sculptor, re–sculptor..
damnable hack.

No wearing prosthetics 'til
phantom reminders

allow —

Who tell him his quads are yet full—aflame
flailing, his flesh, from bone as if..
were still in the midst of
burning his femur
and leaking of
beaches

running..   a child, to chase after dog
and roll in the sand, stuck to his
knees, stuck to the licks
he feels on his toes
where waves
lap

no more.

Feeling it all when bearing the weight
on stilts..   will sit

will sit and roll on wheels 'til then
(get stuck in the surf) —

And mother did stare but
not at his vee, sinews nor brawn

nor soul that reaches down to a sole
wherever those soles be now

nor arms that arc their
alpine peaks when
turning his chair

to greet my mom
who raised the boy
became that man who
drove this friend to meet
his mom, today.

And father did query

"Afghanistan, Soldier?
Or maybe, perhaps, Iran, Iraq.."

Silent. Smiled. Shook the hand and
as we sat, his height again
was bid to say
our grace

(though grace had been there
all along, since first
he said my
name).

"I'd like to thank you
for your son

who brought me here with no charade
and never lets me be the less

I ache to be.

And need to love him
all my life —

I ask
your blessing.

Amen."

doctrinaire

*T*he bend of a neck
betrays
much.

We bow our chin in reverence, drop our head with rue
and woe, the spine will slump midst misery..

tilting, lifting hopeful crown..   relaxing weary vertebrae.
The curve of helix, feel revealed.   Birr exposed.

Each emotion to an angle — be it stooped or straight...

The Angel in the sepulcher let hang his head in quietus..
a forced, familiar solitude.   To the left it barely slipped,
dipped in withered, wondered wan.

The Room was all he'd known for years,
now Walls loomed ever higher.

A lack of ceiling, cloudless whist...
smothered, spitting bits of fire.

'Twas long he saw a starlight's glint,
  or fingernail moon sliver.

  Longer still, a ray of sun,
    no respite, stay deliver..

The Book was always by his side..   Precious little time
didst pass 'tween poring over verse.

  And in the trice he dared look up,
    reveries of when he flew...

    Then gaze wouldst drop and see but Wall,
      couldst swear he saw right through.

        But what?

He kept the will to question hid —
  clandestinely he mused.

    Half–grinning, half–remembering..
      un–knowing, well–confused.

Was there life beyond the Walls?

Written other Books?

Gabriel recalled a soul, whiter plume than even own. Awhile erst, he knew this one.. sylphlike torso seldom clothed.

When Walls were not so high as now

and Book was not so loud .

'Twas time when Angels danced together — sinless, spotless, stainless wings... feathers flying, soaring, sings....

Sooner than their pinions clipped,
ere their clothes were worn and soiled.

Fore their hearts were bled of savor,
palsy served as bliss befoiled..

The Book didst toll its warning peal...
Steeples tripping Cherub's flight.

Seraph falling, crumpled ken,
looming day, adumbral night.

Were *there* amongst the ruins..   Saved by Priests and
Holy Men..   Stripped of quill to spare their souls.

Now Monks and Angels nary vary —— living almost same.

His love of Word, if lifted Spirit,
never height of Walls again.

He wondered whether brick and mortar,
grout and clay betwixt each hymn,

was gravel mixed with Angel fleece...
...halo pieces, plumage, limb.

He thought, of course.. then here must be..
a Heaven's gate.. an ingress free.

— And when and now couldst find no door...
was then and how
dropped head some more.

Dollar Discount

H

e had no means of transport —

Walked charily down the grassy strip that neighbored the shoulderless road —

well–safe from the blacktop's edge, he strode.

Cars zipped by — drivers pressed pedals in great lams of speed — ignoring what twists, with caution — should heed.

Honks from trucks and hightailing pick–ups, with shotgun riders adding their flair — *"Get off the road!"* they'd shout for no reason — as feet angled out their windows for air.

+

Hiked an hour and half, each way.

Ruts, hidden knolls, always were holes — eyes looking down, wary with soles. Watching his steps as they hinted at future, spoke of the now —

were soon striddled past.

Turtles abound and sharing his trek — self–contained homes who suffered no haste — loping along as sauntered, unchased.

Ants astride, too — Egyptian cairns and pyramids tiny, dappled with shades of dirt begird — portals atop with bustle, bestirred.

Then there were snakes, slithering prone — grasshoppers, lizards, dragonflies, mice — all with a story as precious his own —

   and each with a tale told perfectly nice.

+

So *much* to take care, be ginger with toes.
     So *much* to discuss, to share what one knows —

+

Babbled and jabbered and prattled and jawed — the whole of them blathered —

   not one of them bored.

How many the tenets and precepts too rife — too fast the time flew, their pondering life.

As whirring and blurring of autos seemed fade, from dogmas and canons — I fear they all strayed.

Remarking how fate brought them cheerily near, if but for a jiff in their travels, was clear. The boy of our fable, such company, thrilled — the miles he roamed, with flummery — filled.

+

Communed whilst commuting, his verily way — as daily his forage for food — to store.

Sustenance, exercise, friendship
— *du jour.*

doodle
(ditto)

Charcoal me a muscled arm
of bicep–blended might..

shadow–shouldered highlights charm
our torso–tangled night.

~

But what is this that plies me nigh
to yet another man

when easel shouts, *"It's all a lie..!"*
A clone, no better than.

~

Never saw the final sketch
..never hung in frame.

Forever scratching itch of etch
as aperçu the same.

embrace

+

R ood was lost when husk to hide became enmeshed as flesh to glide.. Few, the trices, parched eclipse when KISS betrayed the blistered lips.

Abandon all ye hope survive, as grace bequeathed is flayed alive. More than SPIT from spear and boast would sear the lick of life from host.

+

Let us leave the Bible bound, its parchment inked on hallowed ground. Mud beneath morass and muck, *O Lord..* alloweth he be STRUCK.

If all forsake the Soul of Man, with Son of God an also—ran, then what this Witch and who with TONGUE pervades thy mouth with lance to lung ?

+

+

Cannot breathe but moment's spite when flick of firth doth POUR from bite. Judas craving Him must burn. To fix his Faith must endless learn.

Clear as drench that sepals sip from scourge and whip as lashings drip.   Crown of Thorns and PIERCING breast, stripped of raiment..   claimant blessed.

+

Where flux beguiles writer's pen, such heinous words as these.. *Amen.*   Blasphemy of what was WRIT when Gospel quills were laden shit.

Choose, believe, that death by buss is simply WHITTLED down to thus: Similitude of love is hate.

+

A kiss should carry little weight.

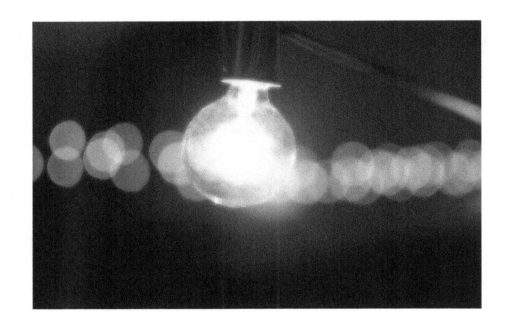

emend

T able for two in a dimly lit room. Film noir setting and tropes.. overhead light swung like a pendulum.

"Would you be willing to testify?"

The lamp's squeak annoyed the shirtless youth. Curl of his lip scowled a silent and nixed reply.

"Answer written questions?"

He swept the yellow pad off the desk. Landed with a thud amidst the floor's ever–pitching shadows. Glared at the seasoned detective.

"Maybe.. shake your head yay or nay when I recount details you might have been privy to. When I'm getting warm?"

Shook his head no, aware of the irony...

smiled at the two–way glass.

:::

Began like most affairs of that particular ilk..

with rich old man and broke young buck hungry for money, Dad, or love. Latter pursuit, rare. All apt here.

"Did the Senator ever speak of his work?"

The tattooed lad flexed a sinewed arm, cracked his neck to the left.. and had there been a nod or shake of his head, the inquisitor couldn't divine.

"Buy you gifts?"

Cracked his neck to the right. Lingering sneer began to fade.

"Expensive things? Cars, baseball teams.. ladies?"

He stood up winged and barbed and, as quickly, obliged again to sit. Interrogator's foot, caught beneath his own, wrested him back to the table and onto his duff. Chair and hustler upended on painted cement.

"She was a friend. I worked corners with her.. Not expensive..

Cheap, like me," he winked.

:::

"Well... getting somewhere. Did she lie about the kid?"

Scrambled to raise self and chair back on their feet...

no easy task with shackles..

"She asked if I could, and I could.
Easy–breezy, bottle 'a gin," he leered.

"Was a beautiful night.   *Did it behind and squinting."*

Sniggered, shrugged..   attempt at humor fell flat.

"He's mine... and hers.."
settled again in the now upright seat.

"We made a choice."

:::

The dick grimaced, loosened his cheap cravat.

"Your choice was selling him to a corrupt politician, with
ties to cartels..

knowing what they traffic in."

He looked more boy than man..   like a high school jock
kicked off the team..   chip on his shoulder, still.

"Not my..   fault..."

Neither believed his swagger.

The one making queries knew well–enough to yield.. as hush often more deft than grill... soliciting replies.

Their last few words lay about.

:::

As if watching a sketch play out before him, the detective's POV was drawn to the motionless brawn.. unmoving and unmoved. Frozen.

Until it wasn't.

With the grace of morning t'ai chi, tendons engaged.. from quiescent to mime, wary the rhythm. Clock on the wall cued the pace. Shackles jingled beneath.

Remembered a night, newborn in arms.. for him it was now. Beaming, the sweat on his face.

Youth cradled a bundle, biceps tensed with relived regard for the pink–jellied flesh writhing and fussing and breathing new life. His brow wrinkled in fidgety awe at the illusory fancy he held.

Now rocking wraith and self. Lips mumbling words.

Somewhere behind us a tiny one's cries turning to coos..

:::

Reverie dallied but moments more....

Enrapt façade appeared buckle..   chimera before him seemed vanish...   our stripling's head caving to bane.

Face, once explored by the quivering paw of a sleepy ball swathed in leather jacket, soon buried in its own wet hands...   bays of a Father who couldn't save his Son.

Tears overwhelmed his orbs, employing near hollows as could, to escape.

:::

A black and white flashback recalled a moment he and the mother presented the child to the celebrious john.. his john..   his child...

their broad grins as proud parents mixed horribly with the truth of giving him up.   But were sure, of course, he'd be raised in a world he and Alice couldn't proffer.

"My wife should be pleased..   I told her the adoption, approved.."

"It's all there," he added as groused.. gruffly passing an envelope.

:::

Back in the room the light had moved from swing to gentle sway, as lull took over the cubicle's drear.

Thought of his Dad and what he did to the boys he raised.

Tracks of soot and dried lament blenched from mien..
rage rouged his strapping lank as chest
and chains began to heave...

Cheek as morphing, melting eye..
bestial expressions slid, slipping off chin..
mouth agape as breath and beatings, sex and boy...

And boy was he and Father, his.. didst spill from lips like blood from cleave..

with spit and spew and spout as flow...

Climaxed in a feral shriek from, lo, his very soul.

:::

"Whatever it takes," his face reset.

Picked up the pad, acceded the pen...

and wrote.

:::

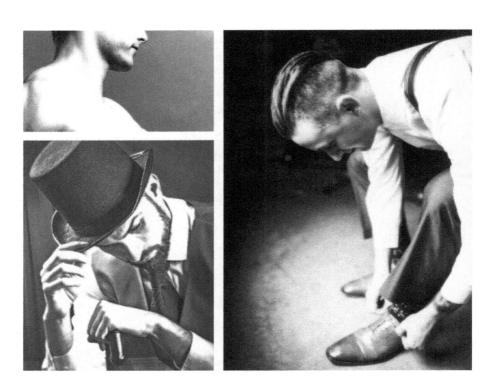

even neck above
(remember warm..   his face)

Always **lips** too honey–steeped.. stealing breath and thieving hours, never really drawn, afloat... round and reaching, poised to wrap my own, my morrows, his. Apartly lazing, grazing press — ply of perfect line and guise to softer, formless, silken weft.

*

Simple almonds, henna jewels of facet–beveled orbs as **eyes**... dark when lumens covet leave, beacons if/when cry for lack. Straight and angled, pining tack, folded ken beneath my nape — almost heart and nigh to art, 'tween bister pools of earth and crest.

Aquiline, but less of arc.. **nose** evinced with pointed flare... heaving heaps of telling slant, nights bespeaking gasp for air. Prophecies preceding grin that herald pharaoh's augured win — ceding scent with balm and breeze.. first to bend when blending mine.

*

Low the rim of banded felt.. **ears** like clay and rimpled shell... carapace of sharded gem, shaped in plaster, tender balanced. Listen well my sweaty pleas in heated trice and rooted moon — rued laments of loss and boon.. hearing ever... open loops.

And **bones** that shape the velvet sheath, hid amongst his chin and cheek, under temple shaping jaw...   strong against the brow and hull as ruling over husk and skull.   With **mane** of scalp and fringe of frons — hair ungoverned, torrent tumbles.   Fur as fountain, overflows.

*

Chasten other, flexion bowed...   sure of wanting should be loved, as cure of wonting would be loved.   To wit, I wish I kissed what saw — and smelled and heard and held in hand.   Spun as sidled **face** to **face** as never looking back..   in place.

ever lose

So off I am blissing, scribing my PROSE,
having a lovely day —

      and damn, doesn't *cadence* prowl.

Little by little it penetrates proofs,
nudged with a stab and
POKE of a stick,

settles between the edits and trims
that marry my *tumult* with
polish and wax —

      betwixting the lines,
           PREGNATING paragraphs.

Bearing their birthing of
jingle and chime —

as PATTER and verse
solicit for,

hmm —

rhyme.

evergreen

O_{nce} again I see that grin,
whitened night we bought a tree
near Lincoln Center, price too dear.
(Lord.. I spent my money then.)

..

Smile you tendered, wild and full,
both beam and branches, me and you.
Proud to bring our sapling home, *our first*,
you led, I trailed...   caboose.

..

Years ago as losing time,
you've built another life..   with him.
Every Christmas, this is mine..
memory I still recall, bleared by

..

wet..   like melting snow.
Turn around and see me carry
trunk, I struggle...   weighs me down
with heady pine and sticky palms.

Wish I carried now.

flesh

At night when holy break their fast,
with miscreants, entwine..

God is pleased with what He cast
and thus was His design.

Would craftsmen ever sweat to forge
such art and function, wed,

then beg their patrons, *"Don't engorge,
or I will smite you.. dead.."* ?

Will burn in Hell forevermore
to char the very skin

fashioned for this very chore,
henceforth libelled.. *'Sin'*.

Where many live a double life
playing hide and seek,

afraid to finger feelings rife.
Flaccid, so to speak.

I counter all this nixing touch,
verboten–branded rot..

Sex is lovely... like it much,
pursue it rather lot.

Maybe folk who fear the fuck
have never done it right.

Immerse thy bits in Godly muck
..and leaveth on the light.

flung

as execrable.

And I rarely lie.. least about vaults from bluffs and escarp—ments. Why, in God's name, would one mislead in so staid a dictum as, *'I hate heights..'* ?

An accursed, odious, damnable slip that left me nigh to losing my breakfast, my lunch, and any and other more nidorous slops — as begged for the light of day.

I resisted their call, kept all in their berth, venue and void... except for the dew that secrets from orbs... their bone and blue iris and penchant for wet. More for the why behind the gambado..

Less for the drop pursuant to dive.

~

To say I was pushed would be too naïve, simple, delusive.

Cajoled, perhaps.. wheedled to dare, maneuvered to lop life with a leap.. saltate myself, gambol right off... rhumba a ruinous crag.

~

The day, akin to the prior profuse, began with first a kiss...
a buss most notable verily for: a complete lack of notability.

Unlike all previous nestles — lips to cheek, mouth, or sundry
this and thats — but for those few/far between instances
when, one or both having applied paste to cuspids, and mouths
otherwise lavingly employed — this smack on the gill was
feigned..   too lax.

The first I ever perceived as sham.

My mien seemed pause, awaiting some clue, as eyes followed
his wake from room.

*"Sleep in, my sweet.   Late for a meeting..   shave and brace..
and then I'm gone."*

No game for the shower, no drop–the–soap which never got
old..   so cute that we shared the spa and sponge these too
many dawns.

Not today.

~

"This afternoon, that thing I broached...."   ashamed to offer
more than that.

He peered from behind the curtain and liner, eyes fronting mirror yet steamed...   pleased with what he saw.

"R..ii...ght..." he tendered cautiously.   *"What time, again?"*

"Six.   You needn't..." I lied.

"Noooo...   of course...   the sky by the face of that monstrous cliff...."

Could see his mind wrangle and swim.   *"Atop or below?"*

He knew my fear of plateaued peaks.

"Upon," I struggled, endeavoring to be heard above the pipes.

His counter was garbled, tangled by torrent and gush, unclear.

I must have drifted asleep.

~

Classes were light on Thursday.   1 o'clock Physics — Lab at 2.

A late lunch with Jane.

"You think the Dean's aware?" she posed, with little room between.. *"It's sooo 'To Sir with Love' and all.."*

I was sure the taco was assembled yesterday, its base soaked through. Still, was the only thing I'd eaten since breakfast. By default, delicious..

"I guess," I barely essayed, withal annoyed how little crunch was left in the shell.

"I mean — Do you raise your hand in class?" she stared wide-eyed at a vision of Lulu and Sydney Poitier flashing cross her frontal lobe's YouTube screen.

"We've been doing this awhile," I averred, *"Feels like..."* the ellipsis seemed hover.

~

Rest of the day, a reasonable blur. 5:30 found me pulling out the University parking lot, noticing his car still in the Faculty grid.

"Whatever," I mused.

~

The precipice rose like a turreted fort scratching the afternoon daze. Fog obscured the tableland's top.

Acropolis veiled by blear.

I worried the kite'd be lost in the mist, the midst of all that smother and smaze.. but there it flew 'pon zephyred brume, too blue and tailed to be bedimmed... forbidding the muffle by murk.

Symbol of my blanketed youth wrapped by one, and only one, who lechered as would lust a pie or buttered crumb with honeyed tea. Shawled by whisp of vapored gloom, too young to cast off beast.

It rose.

~

Free, this diamond — balsa, crêpe and ribboned silk — beautiful prime amongst the stone.

Arete and child's toy. Mislaid, the myth, that held it safe.

~

Enough of the cover of cloud had cleaved. Reddened sky didst

purple the kite.   Reddened sky revealed a face, softer in haze..
younger by years.

"I said I would.." he breathed.

"Why Brother Andrew," I quipped, kissing hard the softest lips,
"I dare not say what I'd rather do than fly this paper bird..."

Could see the frown he'd often sport when I'd add the title fore
his name.   The collar always stiff and tipped, banded white on
ebon shirt, snugly tucked in trousers tight.

A boy of 10 I knew too well — recalled how proud he was to
kneel fore trousers such as these.

Worship   that   which   boys   should   not.

~

"Not much wind," with lowered eyes, *"Not like Spring when
last you flew.. and why, pray tell...   atop?"*

I pondered my riposte.

I'd not done this *'honoring'* in many years — sailing colors
overhead to laurel Aprils lost between my inner boy and

almost man.   And why *upon* the alcazar, not safe beneath its lord and loft —

I had no key for query's plea except I wished on high to be.

"I dunno.."

~

It was more an effort than usual to keep the broadwing plumed on high.   My gift for tugging, running cord, winding round and giving slack the string entwining wooden spool.. fumy, since the time before.

He grabbed my hand.

We circled near the cliffside edge, pulling taut the sisal spun, and managed raise the soaring blue up to a welkin's height.

"I need fly home," I said..

~

"I need be gone and find what's left — no more I shrink from cap and cusp — no more my phobic shunning truth...

flesh of boy is missing youth."

~

Set sail.

Hand released, I spun off side
    and for the moment swore could glide,
        upon a raft of breath and breeze,
            above the rocks and fringe of trees.

And in the time 'twixt endless quiescence and fated descent,
my eyes affixed on his, he spoke —

        or mouthed as moved his lovely lips..

"You got too old."

~

There, as if feathered, pinioned with down — graceless I fell,
ailerons wanting.

Allowing leak the fewest of tears...

maybe for whom
might follow my years.

~

F thru I

Last nite I dreamed of T.S. Eliot
welcoming me to the land of dream
Sofas couches fog in England
Tea in his digs Chelsea rainbows

curtains on his windows, fog seeping in
the chimney but a nice warm house
and an incredibly sweet hooknosed
Eliot he loved me, put me up,

gave me a couch to sleep on..

FEB. 29, 1958

– Allen Ginsberg

fool

R ation out with meted joy,
metered, met with wink and nod..
and left is what I hold inside
(too dear to give too much away).

But what for leavings, weavings woven,
fabric reinforced with glare.
Worn like CLOWN to giveth you

.

a big red nose and funny shoes,
ruffled collar, baggy pants..
and awful jokes to
help you laugh..

AT me, WITH me, NEITHER wins
for both are tied to
who I am.

.

Part I vest you see.

forever 37
(narcissist undone)

Lost again,

I race ahead
whilst reaching back
is catching up.   Am closing in on
someone who

I never was
or knew as me
or ever wanted (then) to be ——

when always thought MORE TIME.

...

Reflecting pool
bespeaking
truth ——

No longer does it
echo folks who
used to lip,

*"Couldn't be
that number, no.
SO YOUNG YOU LOOK!"*

No more.

Unsurprised,
with silent words
they prattle on of other
things.

*Mirror says the same,
but loud.*

...

New, afresh, in place unknown.
CHORES and SWEAT of
younger man.

Maybe toils turn the clock,
bucking tend with prideful trend

—— to bring me back to
when my life was SOMETHING COMING ——
not yet

yet.

...

When *now* was but
an in–between,
before one found one's
field of green.

Then, howbeit, in advance
of all those oats of Life unsupped,
pieces, dreams and parceled shards of
look–at–me–I–matter–much,
as fore us seemed to
hold no crave.

(In fact, I mattered very less

—— until I fixed the parts unsaved,
felt unworthy —

SCREAMED of worth.)

...

Muscles taut and handsome face,
lover, job and home ——

Incomplete.   No more hours.

STILL in future.
GIVE me future.

Smooth of mane and glint in eye ——
Years to work.   Years to write.
YEARS TO RUN
BEFORE I
DIE !

four horsemen

1.

Yellow rays of midday sun
burn with saffron glow.
Thirsty land and tale I've spun
about a man I know.

Came in June one Summer's eve,
eyes alit with flame..
Stayed the season, took his leave
when never spoke his name.

2.

Autumn ambers, embers fall,
trees of blazing rust.
Harvest hennas, auburns all.
He, I didn't trust.

Asked if wanting bestial work
pulling ripened field.
Smiled more a comely smirk...
to him I also yield.

3.

Every shade of Winter white
agleam when said good-bye.
Blizzard promised squall that night
and spawned another guy.

Frosted nose and icy beard
'til warmed him by the fire.
Smell of pine as nigh I neared..
the scent beseemed inspire.

4.

Deliquesce came late that year,
bid apple green peek through.
When birds and buds, as reappear,
my Vernal man didst too.

Gone the Winter whiskered one,
gone the Autumn buck.
Gone the Summer fever fun..

with Springtime left to _____ .

fracas

It's not as if I lied, I thought,
but merely that I spoke —

>   as flouting fed the fight we fought,
>   and there's where I AWOKE.

Head upon a muscled thigh,
eyes were swollen shut,

>   CRADLED in his lap was I
>   — querying the what.

And how and why and if it's TRUE,
the promise that he made,

>   *"To win the heart that beats in you."*
>   A verbal hand grenade.

"I never made a motion toward
the who I knew you were.

       Those from you were well–ignored."
My head was still ABLUR.

For what seemed like a mix of verse,
from innocent to rough —

       EXPLODED then from bad to worse
       when words were not enough.

Neither wrestled fair, I fear,
with fisticuffs engaged.

       Viewed askew through blinking blear
       — our roil grew ENRAGED.

i i

ii

"And I'm supposed to waive away
the wending of your will —

      so NOW you think it's A–OK
      to let you have your fill!"

Breathless hush, surveilling field
of battle, black and blue,

      bruises, bangs — began to YIELD.
      "I guess I always knew."

And though, I'm sure, is not my aim,
my resoluteness slips,

      knowing how he feels the same —
      a MELD of blended lips.

ii

Fran

I

think was a Wednesday

and you gave me sox..   Why gift? Why sox? I might
wonder now...   seems what we did then.

Red, white and gray —   thick, crunchy cotton we
wore in the 80's.

Partook margaritas...   Prosciutto and pasta...
Played the piano...   Pet Shop Boys crooned.

My stomach was jumpy..   even with Alex, your cat,
in my lap.

: :

Was then you sat near, your slat back chair nigh —
it, facing backwards..   *you,* facing me..

with both us too close..   warm, I felt breath —
mingled ours, garlic..

kissing me hard and feathered, same time —
searching, familiar...

'tween us, no air —

I, still, may be there.

Friends
(of Summer, simple verse)

August 1946 —

Sun and sand, a sleepy mix.

Met in June on double date..

John and Mary, Bill and Kate.

...

Mid—July, a barbecue..

John got drunk as Bill did too.

Took a break from chasing skirts —

Shedding caution, shucking shirts.

...

Nothing more, not much to tell..

Coming under nother's spell.

Love is love as ocean waved —

Need not judgment, nor be saved.

full of it
(SBD)

To be so clever, rich with words,
as never venting stink..
when all thy verse unwraps, begirds,
with parchment prettied ink.

I simply know of this and that
and all of else is moot.
Allow me add that what I shat
this morning...   absent toot.

*

So he who scripts such florid fluff
might barely make a sound
whilst pinching loaf, your magic duff..
with umber trending brown.

Hush, I say, you wretched imp,
perfection not my fault.
My piss is even golden limp,
as bard and bowl exalt.

If what you say, albeit crass,
is, more to point, a crow.
Equating words with wiping ass...
a knack for ode and 'go' ?

> *You and all your jealous scribes*
> *will ever covet wit.*
> *Mine is flush..   and all your gibes*
> *but prove you crave my shit.*

*

Is clear you wish to prove your worth,
please take this well in heart.
Seems your ken for pen lacks mirth
and stifles how your fart...

> *Yet we chat at length of quill,*
> *in limericks you speak.*
> *And somehow blend it all with swill*
> *...*

..you scatologic freak.

*

gelid event
(never say never)

8 degrees, Fahrenheit.

Dad would take all us kids
to a tundral Jones Beach
(Long Island, New York)..
their Star Gazing Nights.

Always seemed Winter, ever hot chocolate, marshmallow minis
— lectures inside on yonder to Galaxies, Cosmos, and why.

—

Driving through the ebon that night, Dad pointed to stars,
as told (retold) the Gift of the Magi, the glim in the heavens...
been only a month since Christmas Eve.

He added tonight was clear like that..
                    night baby Jesus was born.

Closing my eyes, a little boy plea (for Father and Christmas)
"..live longer than me."

—

All of his sons,
plus more from the neighbors,
poured out the doors and
trunk of the wagon...
'58 Chevy Bel Air.

And filled up on cocoa and leftover cookies...

listened to words — the Northern Lights — how beautiful were
— indescribable, rare.

Aurora Borealis....

Tiny, the hope, of seeing them live.   Orator guy made it
well–plain..   They *never* came down..   *"Not this far South..."*

After the descant, out for a gander the Little, Big Dippers..
under the stars (and into the frigid) we went.

—

Too small for the telescope set up outside, relying on brothers'
spirited telling of comets and flickers, their twinkles and gleam
— adding their ooh's, peppered with aah's — especially ardent
to heighten my green.

So cold.   Did I mention?

Couldn't stop shaking...   in hand–me–down coat with sleeves
way too short..

> *when Dad swept me clean,*
> *all goose bumps and woolens,*
> *lifting me high, square*
> *on his shoulders...*

something he'd done — not since I was three.

"Look up!"

Now, above brothers, o'er the damn telescope, warmly against Father's big head....

> *Seemed like a springing*
> *the umbra stood singing..*
> *from colorful sprites*
> *came whispers and lights...*

silence and secrets and speaking in tongues —

—

Ribbons ablaze like blizzards aglow
> *'twixt runnels of teal with turquoise aflow..*

'neath showers of gold, nigh shadows of pink,
> *serpents of amethyst slithered their slink.*

And stars amid mizzle that swept 'cross the vast
> *were flung by the Angels, as if had been asked..*

wending their way into heart and up nose,
> *appealing for sanctum, our soul and some toes —*

— I answered with *'yes'*.

Grabbing my legs,
Dad, raising me higher,
began to fly
'tween sips and slips
of cocoa and sky....

midst hues and blues from wings of a Muse..
feathers that fell, full—under her spell.

Miracle night, forever within —   as Father now, too.

—

Dad set me down with glove wrapping mitten..   as headed
inside..   the freezing we fled..   a little more cocoa..

"...like Christmas," he said.

—

GGWG

N

o one sees inside of you.   No one knows the reasons why those like us might secret thus —

why Angels carry guns.

Allowing for no fully fleshed–out, grande exposition, as owing to the subject's need–to–know stricture, permit me to elucidate abstrusely:

He (that be the He, forever, set off with an 'H') promised nothing when we took this fell crusade — no reward nor recompense. All us Cherubs volunteered.

"It may be but a folly, mine. Lord knows.." (chuckled as He uttered those paired words and every time He hijacks human tropes — in specie and especially those that cite Himself)..

"Lord knows.. (repeated, recovering) *I've given those protlopastic, inelastic, orgiastic creatures..* (self–appointed master of internal rhyme, we often roll our eyes as well) *every benefit of the doubt."*

"Still....
    (does like spawning pauses)

       Perhaps one more."

We were bundled together like bales of cotton, feathers more apt — en masse we assembled as if were roped, clustered, kibitzing in the transport room's lobby.

Clouds convening out dormers and portholes signaled a mighty storm coming.

I was quite convinced 'twas His behest the Cumulonimbi were summoned. Prone to the dramatic, He frequently orchestrates vainglorious backdrops, theatrical ambience of inordinate compass, lofty largesse for all such events of coalesce — where one populace is stirred with another.

And here, affirmed, a citizenry commingling was tout–de–suite–ly imminent.

Inasmuch as Earthlings and Seraphics were amongst His favourites (though I never understood His fondness for us, the latter, considering Lucifer and his/our ilk's early and exigent divergence from brand).. going balls to the wall with the fanfare that night struck me as more so...   even than usual.

———

Wasn't long ere deafening rumbles and pealing rolls shook the chamber, rattling karma and roiling chi — harried halos more brilliant by bolts — lightning strobes in toto too close for this faerie's comfort. (I must make mention said labored bravura our next Union meeting)...

A thousand Nagasakis blithely bursting
                          round a flock of lambs.

Corybantic choir voices filled the gaps 'tween crashing claps and crackling booms of wrackful, wreckful thunder.   I'm certain much of the dirge piped in was borrowed from *"2001"* —

the Monolith Scene — could get you the link.   (God as devoted Kubrick fanboy).

Midst zig–zag blazes knifing clefts cross the sky, aurora colours frescoed clouds like smears of a brush sated and sodden with pigment on well–steeped plaster.   Fanning out in inky swells, they streaked our wings with oil–sheened rainbows, through lavaliered prisms, hung from His neck.

———

Our numbers were called, weapons conferred, missions attuned, pinions unpinned, uniforms tailored and tweaked.   Mine, the garb of a teacher, professor, or kin to that breed... imagined the Dean of some fancy College, Literature spewing from whole of my pores...   though likely, I thought, some Middle School tutor in Texas or Tucson or Timberland Creek.

We'd been readying for weeks..   honing our skills, perfecting our aim, developing deftness in all situations — now in possession — our very own guns.

Armed and ammoed, dressed and adroit, wingless and wondering, we gathered in queues in front of each gateway, each to a region. Mine was America, somewhere, a State, central and south.

And outside the bastion, tempest now silent — unnervingly so — did little to quell the whirling within..

—

Whooooossh....

the hatch opened, an ebony airstream vacuumed me in (as Black Holes seem quite rightly named)... a moment of dropping, flailing my wings (phantom indeed), legs did a jig like pedalling a bike.. as if that would break my fall...

—

El Paso.

Good Gabes with Guns.

Fell easily into routine. Found my Prius fun to drive, teens I find exhausting...

and so much more to read, been written, since I was a Pupil. Thrilled to know that Shakespeare still (must share with him upon return) ad rem....

..read with phones that sub as book and pen and ink and stage, and yet — than more confusing, all of that —

will multi–task as friend.. (?)

———

Sueded patches cushioned elbows, hands supported chin, gazing out behind my desk at Students untangling their Final Exam. On these I look most fondly — those under my apprentice.

Thirteen years they lived a life, prurient and prying...

equal parts, things of worth, an awful lot of stuff more droll. Reminded me of me, that age.

'Twas yesterday — seems, I too, disported skin where crêpe now swags tween cheek and eye and other breadths.

"Where did those 4,896 years go.." I mused, mumbling.

———

Gathering papers, wishing Good Summers, wistful the months I'd spend alone.   No plans for vacation, budget nil...   Heaven is tight with per diems.

Closing the car door, both real and symbolic, was grateful I'd not yet been tested.   Safe was the schoolyear, teachers and children.   Almost forgetting the gig...

...when a cerebral Post–it note prompted — was low on milk and sundries — a Walmart pit–stop well in order.

———

"Too many browns!" wailed under his breath — like a howling lyric from metalhead's throat, stanzas screamed but hardly heard.   Fellow shoppers ignoring his plea.

Perhaps he was seeking a tin of tan polish...   for loafers or boots (the latter his stomping implied)....   could only find bister.

Me, more concerned with keeping my shopping cart from veering into clearance displays, its rear wheels unruly, clicking and scraping their mutinous intent — I sailored on, oblivious of much else.

Yet, behind me perceived a brisk about–face...   same strident steps making way back to front of the store, toward the doors, with me assuming..   his vehicle parked outside.

Perhaps he forgot..   *"bags*, of course,"   I divined out loud.

The observation came and went.   Now where are those fruit cups..   what aisle the angel hair pasta?

Seeking to discharge monies owed, I struggled with my MasterCard, inserting, sliding, nothing worked. Nametag emblazoned, my cashier, Nahla, smiled her surmise, *"Slide it quick and easy, Shug. You're not alone... this reader skews possessed."*

Or maybe said, *"It's fucked."* I did quite like her nails.

Completed, receipted, I gave my thanks with a weighty, *"God bless."* Contritely turned to view a line, the one I no doubt inspired with my unforgiving debit ineptness.

———

Faces, almost to a one, aghast... most miens motionless... some, whose eyes seemed losing life, leaned on shoulders front of them... then crumpled to their shoes. All those *'pops'* that blended with the bings and snaps and bells from the register — I thought precisely usual —

proved not banal at all.

I spun back to Nahla, collapsed behind her station. Daubs of blood drooled and dribbled round the black conveyor belt, carrying smeared groceries o'er and past a loudly beeping scanner — dropping them, unbagged, on her spiritless form.

Seconds stretched my prose to verse, as prattled thoughts were swept in runes.   Silent musings writhed and rhymed (spartan, like an ode)...

Corners of my eye did stray..
    children from my school.
        5 were there and on their way
            to swim in Berto's pool.

Two were buying Promise Rings
    (I heard it first last week).
        Puppy love in June, it sings,
            but now wouldst never speak.

And twins with birthday gift in mind
    for other, thought alone.
        Separate came to seek their find.
            Which one dead..   unknown.

Fifth has taste of salt and blood,
    forever..   staining lips.
        Fresh, the wound and bullet's flood
            on fresh, his bag of chips.

I flung around to face where eyes of others now be fixed..

———

As trained, and yet with adlibbed tact, battling disquietude, grabbed my pistol.. leathered sling, slung beneath my blazer. Lifting arm, aimed the piece in increments, as if Da Vinci's *'Vitruvian Man'* himself were clad in corduroy.. and I was but the puppeteer.

Barrel ticking unseen notches. Target followed forward, toward, leading from the gun's front sight. Finger pulled the trigger soft, could hear the digit's knuckle crack, as time and tour stood still. Until..

Sonic boom of muffled blast

as cannon plumed a muscled past.

Blur from muzzle followed flash, as he who faulted *'browns'* too rife, squibbed from forehead hole his Life. Rifle yielding, palm now slack, slipping grip to cede attack. Clough I cleaved in wailing pout, which whiplashed neck neath gobbet spout — collapsing knees and more to floor — didst pool his scarlet liquid like a laurel wreathing tress.

And just like that, a job well done, reversely drawn through starless hole, debriefing as I went.   Gone were plaid and credit cards, Prius clicker, pasta sauce.   Back were wings and gloried robe —

and gun I left at Gate.

———

I greeted Nahla, others too, easing their transition — was helpful that we'd met on Gaia — explained their fate, allayed their fears, palliating tears...

The children I embraced until their trembles turned to *O–M–G's* — swaying, reeling, wheeling 'bout — greenhorn group of gasp and gulp as whirled their dervish gaze.

Handing out of halos stirred a spate of *"Who me?"* protest glee (and arbitrary frisbee toss).   Meting feathered fluff, their raiments flowing, followed thus...   eliciting a flux, a flood...   a flurried flush of airborne selfies.

I promised each their family, friends would join them here anon..

When time illumes a feckless clock
with moments kindled light.

Memory as future tense, Auld Lang Syne
to every night.

Where clouds will hold your soul aloft, beneath
your feet a glow..

guns and rifles drip their wax upon the
flaming flesh below.

Faint the cries of burning eyes
as leaden barrel's
melt is

felt.

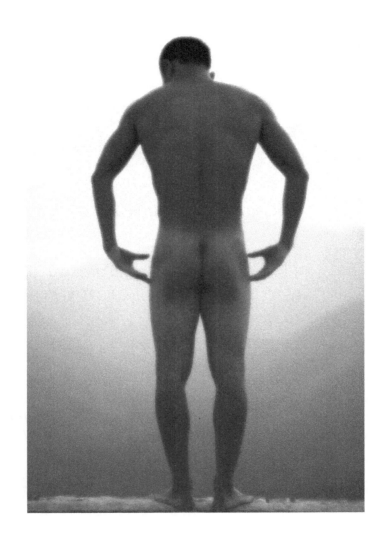

gleaning camber
(locker room)

H

e lacked a certain symmetry.

With CROOKED nose from sparring youth, albeit hook of meager cant, he nonetheless was not a one you'd think was thought a sprite..

III

Yet there they were, plain as plume, ailerons of feathered puck, but these adjoined to naked buck whose THIGHS and buttocks would not stop besetting me an oddly way. Re of this could not dismiss, as led a mind et al. astray.

Failing to ignore his lure, skew of beak and breadth of brawn, when bid anew with bended view, his more UNHIDDEN flesh and thew.. soon nudging part of self (yes, that) to rise and firm and, owing thus, didst ruin line of towel, mine..

I I I

Where I stood with Mark of Cain, roused for all the world to see, noting who my eyes held rapt (though ogling, I think more apt) was UPPING that which would not tuck, as furthering my terry swell... betrayed the fond I felt.

And curved, it is, that makes for bulge, I bid thee heed,

my words, indulge. Leaning slue (like some of you),

slight of yaw (if light in awe), doth speak afresh of

SYMMETRY (and no, the twisted irony is not a thing

that's lost on me)...

I I I

And truly now INFLATABLE

when not at all debatable.

Relatable, I posit here...

is arcing like his nose.

glim

He slowed to a lean, as barely alive.. looking well past.. to heavenly visions, a corner, the dive...

- At likely those kissing, their love again new, in trough they first met.. first jism they blew.

- Or speaker upbearing a go–go boy's throb, as eardrum and grundle seem evenly robbed.

- Else fragrant graffiti, the piss–painted wall, and he that be proud of his manner of scrawl.

More cursory swivel than twine of the nape..   as tried
to assay...   which of these 3 held more of his sway.

By time I'd unwound he'd crossed the 12 feet,
up the small step from dancefloor to meet...

Now inches between his and my face,

> *"Lazy eye, mine..*
> *was <u>you</u> that drew gaze."*

I let that sink in
fore queried with grin,

midst grinding and grabbing as
probing for lack,

"Other parts equally, languidly slack... ?"

glue

And as it was on Christmas Eve,
   their yearly Ball of Balls,

bleeding Vogue and make–believe
   with tinsel–lavished walls..

He had the gown, the only one,
   its rubies hung in drips

on evergreen with sequins spun...
   All that, and bag of chips.

*

Neckline plunged and skirt lay bouffe,
   his wig was piled high..

shoes, Dior, and like Tartuffe,
   their label was a lie.

But who doth care when oozing luxe
   and gushing grace and charms.

All these things and rings cost bucks...
   He finished shaving arms.

Applied a bit of eau de this
     when added eau de that,

a combination musk and kiss
     and pussy (i.e. cat).

Squishing manhood, tucked away,
     whilst other flesh he fluffed

as much as could for bustier...
     though sparsely was it stuffed.

                    *

Touches left, but velvet gloves
     with beads and bracelets chose..

feet in shoes with push–and–shoves,
     the evening not for toes.

Stole of mink, of course was faux,
     brooch upon it, pinned..

paste for jewels, but who would know...
     His matching earrings, twinned.

Floating out the open door,
    his basement flat was cheap..

beneath the Dollar Discount store,
    the steps were snowed in deep.

Stiletto heels do help a lot
    with keeping hemlines dry..

Madonna would have turned back... *NOT !*
    He raised his skirt to thigh..

        *

...to hail a cab this wretched night
    of blizzard mixed with sleet,

beggared carriage nigh in sight..
    He focused on the street.

Knew his way through darkest cracks
    and crannies, to be sure..

a shorter course, he could relax....
    his worries premature.

Through alleyways and unlit lanes,
  whilst wearing but a gown...

perhaps unsafe, the fact remains,
  would help him hie, cross town.

Teeter–tottered, swiveled, swished,
  wobbled, wavered, stopped.

Assessed the route, a prayer he wished....
  and then, abruptly, plopped.

*

Crinoline didst break his fall,
  tangled 'low the tulle..

heel was broken, hope was small,
  the Angels' whimsy, cruel.

For these were but the perfect pumps
  to complement his dress...

Fate doth deal us scrapes and bumps,
  but this....   a holy mess.

"I GOT !" He heard, a cheerful cry
    from somewhere 'neath a tarp..

as wondered what it meant and why,
    listened further, sharp.

"Epoxy, dahling.. instant gunk,
    the kind that dries too soon..."

Didst pull our lovely out his funk.
    He gathered up the strewn..

*

...that lay upon the slush and snow,
    his wig and heel and clutch.

He thought with glue and off he'd go...
    would not be late, too much.

Scrambled up as if were on
    a frozen pond of ice,

slipped and slid and thereupon..
    "...Your offer, very nice."

For nothing ever kindly mild
    happened to our lad,

heretofore and more, reviled..
    Child prone to sad.

Oft alone, fearing those
    who questioned why he cared

for feathers, frocks and frilly clothes....
    Polite ones only stared.

            *

But most were not at all that sweet
    to solely glare with eyes,

wouldst break his heart and bones complete,
    and revel in his cries.

Cast away by folks and friends,
    he forged another life,

turning tricks and odds and ends...
    His isolation rife.

When from behind a cardboard box
the faerie didst appear

with soiled clothes and tattered sox
and sightless eyes, I fear.

*"Feel free to search my shopping cart,
I think it's near the front..*

*I heard you fall and felt it smart...
It's there, you'll have to hunt.*

*

*"Oh I remember in my youth,
would walk divine in heels..*

*You need some money?   Tell the truth...
How you fixed for meals..?"*

And all at once, a darkened mass
of shifting shadows rose..

frightened first, the dread didst pass...
He wrinkled up his nose.

Not so much for clash of scent,
    his florid vs. piss,

but more with grin, their good intent.
    "It seems I've been remiss...

Meet the ones I share my space,
    my very closest kin.

On Christmas Eve, and just in case,
    we gather here, within..

*

"...for never know if year from now,
    the family that we made....

friends and strangers..   here we bow
    for blessings left unpaid."

Asudden in a flurried flash,
    a flush of festive fuss,

fire lit in barreled trash...
    with chestnuts roasted thus.

Whilst candles glowed in paper bags,
    this moonless, starless night...

were no resplendent gifts with tags,
    no tree bedecked in light.

No baubles, bangles, graced the brick,
    no swags of wreath and fir..

but snow didst manage do its trick...
    sans frankincense and myrrh.

*

A manger scene of boxes piled
    and feral cats as lambs,

homeless Mary, Joseph, Child...
    Cheetos, lieu of yams.

But what was missing seemed be slight,
    no Fête was greater than....

I swear that Santa stopped his flight
    when dancing first began.

Salsoul Christmas disco aire
    with boom box throbbing bass,

in broken heel and wigless hair
    and Conga Line in chase....

He taught the Vogue to those who cared,
    inciting others Twerk...

shared a joint when Tangoed, paired
    and screamed, *"YOU BETTER WORK !"*

                    *

Hostess, blind, was pouring brew,
    all spill and dribbled hugs..

mostly nog and rum, as too,
    was ripple sluiced from jugs.

Mistletoe was making rounds...
    when seated by her side,

our stripling teasing kissy sounds.
    Our server's smile wide.

To match her blush our fancy lad
    applied a gleam of gloss,

shadow, liner, powdered tad..
    Milady at a loss...

"Clearer than my vision young
    when erst my eyes could see,

I welcome you, my daughter, son...
    our Land of Let It Be."

*

No one found the glue that night,
    no heel was ever fixed..

the Ball, it seemed, an oversight
    as if the Gala nixed.

Somehow in the all of it
    forgotten, some might guess,

as found a World, a Home, to wit...
    the night I wore a dress.

good patrician
(isomorph)

+

Divining will as long before
this PEERLESS, seeming, face I wore.

Viewed aloft from lambent fray,
an offered glimpse — a versed ballet.

+

Neck of swan and lucent blues
with eyes unclouded, clearest hues —

Blazing 'neath the polished skin
as when was borne and HARDLY BEEN.

+

+

Facsimile of who I am
coalescing — wolf and lamb.

A BLENDING of the then and now,
minus youth, that sacred cow.

+

Under breast and lining womb,
the dreams that lie in WAITING ROOM.

Castles razed and battles won —
if noble voyage yet begun.

+

+

SCARCELY KNIGHTED, rarely fought —
new the image, skin untaut.

Armor wrinkled, virtues bare
as steed replaced by comfy chair.

+

Will focus camera, needful of
the fawning shadows — fuzzy 'bove.

Wellborn King of tilted stance,
LIGHT THROUGH SCRIM, a courtly dance.

+

hard
(for him)

It wasn't the end I thought would be,
if dub it a start, misleading thee..

a veer, perhaps, a fork that led
to rutted, gutted, *"More!"* he pled.

An unpaved road of tortured whim

      pocked with hoofs, this luring djinn.

Mocked my trim as laid the blame,
by which I ceded gracile frame..

baring soul that stumbled long
the side of spur.. my thinly song.

Slender braced in balanced crawling,

      bloated gird could topple, falling.

Neither cocked nor surly swaggered,
up to snuff, as tending laggard..

'til I donned that helmet forged,
atop my dome (of soft/ engorged).

Similitude for what is both:

    Words that curse and pledge of oath.

Ever–feigning..   now and forward,
pliant soul as leaning toward..

CODPIECE bolted, blazing LANCE,
flaccid HEART defying stance.

Metallurgic, cast and built,

    molten silver..   ferric gilt.

Soldered weight of
muscled plait..

buff encrusted
one too late.

Time I spent at gym to please..

afore my lover...   *other knees*.

hawk & barter

Was a face
across the mart
mid merchandise of
à la carte

and where I sat
as morning–eyed
enrapt upon and on
would ride —

Village fountain, fresco wall
me atop a crumbling all

apportioned 'twixt the blush and pall.

+ + +

Cobbled street
and coin–strewn mortar
low the gush

— and rush of air

above the treasures
feet were there —

Ghostly line
(that severs spine)

extending from the top of crag
and through my very soul —

Nearly splitting God and sky
as sundered me in two

unwhole.

+ + +

That which proves my proof of ill

from that which Father raised — until.

+ + +

Silver, gold and glinting eye
of he who leers below
the spray

— greenish slime, adjacent gray

with pretty, tendered
burnished clay

the many years of wet
wear down
those shiny bits
of hope and prayer —

Could buy me food
(and what would trade)
from sellers in
our village square

their smooth of etching
polish, gleam

— leaders that have died, unclean
render wishes, tzars
of sleight —

He of portrait
lumened, bright

and he, too, beaming
bids me wonder

how so under folded light.

+ + +

As coin unminted
fingered smooth

years of smile, turning tricks
my potentate

of leaning bricks —

Shaded eyes to starboard aft
body built to proffer
craft

third to decade, still the face
(and other filling) someone new

— as out of sun, beyond the wares
if almost hidden

well in view.

+ + +

Twisted halfly
peeled to waist
hands would pose

where poised among

to highlight 'tween what
pockets, hung

as seemed too grand
a force be rolled
— for words I brand or

trousers hold —

Would guise and grab
the side it
lay

was then I chose to enter fray.

+ + +

From market's vending
— left my perch for

eager feeding
hungered search —

Not for harvest seasoned sweet
(a morrow this, was sure
could eat)

but other thirst, another meat.

+ + +

Nay, with coins from fountain's well
but whispered verse

and spin I'd sell —

history repeats

Prescient crest to capstoned CUSP that leads believe the forward scrum. Meridian of offing's MORROW. Chordal lyres STROKED to thrum.

" " "

PAST portends the herald's bode, totem augur sooths his say. Brass will STRUMPET parchment's paean. Fate DIVINED by démodé.

humble

To benefit the small in me, I built a tiny
  house.   My heart exists outside, a tree,
      as shelter.. bird and mouse.

Blushing fruit and modest nest, plum the
  branches bid.   Orchard wee with me as guest
    ..life is meek amid.

Hobbit home with elfin yard, blooms that lead to
  door.   Sky above is plenty starred...
    no one 'neath is poor.

: : :

Window open, vista vast, view from where
  I quill.   Tell you this (though no one asked)
    ..lowly me has skill.

Vexing verse as penning prose, pressing sonnets
  sing..   sheepishly, with words composed
    of rhythm, rhyme and swing.

Core I be with simple glee, a garden gnome
  in specs.   Giving thanks for hearth and key
    ...and what I'm writing next.

husk

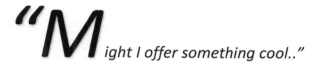*ight I offer something cool.."*

I tendered, canvas 'tween.

—

Longest time his hand lay raised, as if the air itself unsure..
When hence deemed through as flex of thew,
urged to keep it thusly, prayed —

for twisted lumens, bicep taut.

Until his fingers opened, more unfurled,
unwrapped, and splayed —

—

"I think I'm well...

Presume be shorn of shorts, again?"

Knew the drill and still would rouge
          fore every pose of bare and near.

As hung, the gloves, behind him swayed..   with nape of
neck in gilded frame competing for my palette smear —

Front as back endeavored, fought,
sparring me my bid.

—

Silent boy with stomach flat and yielding pecs,
          purview plied —

Limbered pigment, brush and lithe, ye wonders whereby
paint his glow..

As send two willing eyes to fall.   What cleaves above to
formless low — beneath that finds one apt to show,
as patch of hair and nether down — easel hides
(but he doth not).

Lingers glim — of staring, glaring, daring camber rise.

To Ovid lips and Roman nose o'er shoulders chiseled,
angles forged.   Whittled drifts of sculpt and carving,
hew of hands to harden, hold an ever–slowing heart —

and all the other things I bleed,
    if only could such things be cede.

  —

But now with gaze of model's whist
      an artist mustn't fix — too deep.

His brow and lids unmoved amidst
      a breath of hum and kiss — asleep.

To keep, the canvas in–betwixt...
      'til palette blue is twilight mixed.
          When boxer wins as fight resumes
            and ebon lights the dauber's room.

I feed them

And as I kneel on frosted grit,
bestill before a homeless cur..

She licks the paper bowl I hold,
stable, able get each drop.

Morsels missed when no one cared,
allowed their hands be lapped and nibbled..

Trusting of my alms oblation,
nothing sweeter, grateful graze.

Now to heaven as we lay
head to head when eye to eye..

Cold the gravel early March,
neither seems to notice midst..

Kissing nose 'tween folded palms,
salvo hers to snuggle, nudge..

If only I could take them home,
feast and fire warm..   'til then...

' '

I hold the paper bowl again.

' '

I like bad boys

U nknowable, an evil mix
of NOT and that which lures —

I love a thing I cannot FIX,
untenable the cures.

PILLAR posing, pissing wall,
I will not look away —

swollen grope, my skin doth CRAWL.
Flee, I should, but stay.

—

RUE the nerd with all his heart
who begs me for a word —

I listen but a world apart
when ALL bespoke unheard.

Tongue and spit UNSNEER the lips
as taunt and tease belie —

is me but drool of sorry drips
with nice one wailing...   'WHY?'

I thru L

i am a beggar always
who begs in your mind

(slightly smiling, patient, unspeaking
with a sign on his
chest
BLIND)yes i

am this person of whom somehow
you are never wholly rid(and who

does not ask for more than
just enough dreams to
live on)

I AM A BEGGAR ALWAYS

– E. E. Cummings

in a name

Often hard to find the switch
to bandy 'bout, discover which —
is wielded at that very wink

when pen to parchment, ere to ink.

Leaving me to channel sprite
or brawny spectre, pinioned flight —
Scales of dragon, taloned beast

or sweet the Seraph, nigh to Priest.

+

Presented with the choice of these
and driven by a need to please —
I beg of you to guide my quill,

tack my turns and siphon, fill.

Muse of luz or dun of soul
marshal strength of pith and knoll —
Allow me entrance, hidden lair.

Stake your bid..   my noms de guerre.

in process

W

as raining hard.

Clutching her brolly with white–knuckled fists, round the brick corner, hitting a wall of tempest and clout.. nylon gave way as folded the metal in half. Blunted–ly dumped, flung down an alley.. continued her press with pelt and gale.

Scrabbling inches each hat–held stride, advanced toward the building's marquee — promise of shelter, at least, from the douse.

———

Right side tucked 'neath canopy's gilt.. the Limo, parked..

and rocking.

A gentle sway, the rhythmic cadence of well–rhymed verse — pattered, insistent —

She couldn't help but wonder with grin.

Entertained a myriad whys, its deliberate reeling side to side.. easily culled to a few.. most involving plasm and flesh.

The sidewalk was empty, no one but her would brave the buffet, the batter of wet — defined the city's late afternoon.

Lit up a smoke, her last of the day (except for the balcony draws before bed). The rain's trajectory, angled descent, more plumb to the street, wind far more restrained.

With first inhale head filled with fuzz.. been hours since the after–lunch. Her gaze soon glossed as settled her pry... the Stretch's black windows.

As if it were summoned, perform for her stare, one suddenly cracked an inch. Up again half and down maybe two — closing, it rose, dropping some more —

———

Continued to yo-yo, bobbing in tempo, surging with Cadillac's pitch. When STOPPED. Glass now nearly fully agape.. whimpering, ended its bounce.

Though dark in the well, the canopy lights behind her gave aid.. silhouettes edging those within.. painting a pair in Limo too still.

One sat up as roundly illumed.

Wiping his mouth, looked out from the dim. Spit something frothy destined for curb.

"Pops, your foot, whacked us a button.. Got us a freak."

The other now glaring as bolted upright —

An old man's dick is hard to miss, wrinkled and quaggy, even when not. He zipped up his fly (catching some flay — his yelp would imply).

As reaching over the shirtless youth, wincingly cudgeled and toggled a switch, ending our smoker's free burlesque show.

———

Her back to the caddy, feigned disregard, loudly found humming something from *"Cats"*.. drug her last drag.

She giggled what witnessed, the titter short–lived as thought of her own... Son the same age.

Limo took off like shedding its skin.

Half a block down it came to a halt. The young boy appeared almost thrown out. Gathered himself, door slammed behind. As car, once more —

Hied again, stopped.   Was cast out a shirt.

Then Cadillac lost in the spate.

Dug into his jeans.. releasing the phone wedged
in the squeeze.   Wearing his sark like a Sheik
in the rain, thumbed the address furbished in gold..
the building's marquee.

———

Twisting enough to catch the boy's glim, flicking her
cigarette, aiming for street — slapping her entrance,
shuffling stiff —

revolving door seemed rowel her through.

Frightened somehow, though not sure why.. bent on
pulling loose the skirt..   still stuck with rain to shivering
knees —

———

inspired by a vinyl word

S tay the stirred moiré mid–swirl,
scratched and scored with claw.

SOMETHING wends its flourished whirl —
gleams bespeaking awe.

><

LEAVING HOME doth wipe the plate
of wirra witch at work —

but cedes a spin that curries fate.
Alive in feast and cirque.

><

Riddance of adumbral scrim —
JUDE in shadowed vale.

Shooting stars will scar the dim
when comets blazon trail.

Simple thing, this upward glance —
empyreal, its orbs.

REVOLUTION smooth they dance,
reflect what black absorbs.

><

Beneath the dust of ancient moon,
beside the NOWHERE MAN,

below the lilt, a Beatles' tune —
betwixt what they began.

><

Furl affixed as Fab the Four,
a plain recall of past.

Ever young, their scrape is yore —
WALRUS versed in vast.

><

LUCY IN THE SKY tonight
with diamonds   — heaven etch —

As I attempt, IMAGINE, write
and twist this tale I stretch.

interlude

ii

Only a gash, I'm sure wasn't me,
and what if it was? *Unwitting*, you see.

Made worse falling down as smacking her head.
That was on her.. the plentitude bled.

Was only a whore, a nigger, *a fag*,
a ladyboy dressed up in lipstick and drag..

Still alive, right? Indictment with hitch.
As yet can't be blamed for killing the bitch.

ii

i i

Dress was *all fancy*, apart where I tore it
when grabbing her stuff..   How proudly she wore it.

Lousy at head.   *So graceless*, in fact,
I paid her with crowbar, the talent she lacked.

As swung from behind..   my hand maybe slips..
for touching my dick with fingers and lips.

Rose from the brick midst *cower and crawl*.
Lovely her nails whilst clawing the wall.

i i

O, why doth she cry as limp on my shoulder?
Begging for mercy. *Praying* I hold her.

Locked on her eyes (before they lost light),
I thought of my kids.. *their own twice as bright.*

"Lady or who, whatever you be,
YOU ASKIN' FOR HELP?" Now wordless her plea.

"Get offa my suit..! Got blood on my shirt..!"
Wadded up twenty, her crumpled in dirt.

irriguous

City smudged in oil paint,
canvas steeped with blazoned blear.

Fresco gilt, enfeebled, faint,
woozy sweeps of drab and drear.

Languid traipse with fluid fix,
stippled gloss on concrete square.

Blending daubs when melting bricks,
cobbled streets of slick and pare.

. . ..

Impressionistic camera lens..
palette, easel, soup for one.

Sprinkle, spewing, spitting, cleanse,
brolly over, pining sun.

. . ..

Bleeding vapors, smazing gaze,
frame the point of view that vaults.

Golden hues in silver greys,
spanning years, an oozy waltz.

. . ..

. . ..

Metaphors to enter musing,
psalm and drizzle mizzle murk.

Puddles winning, shoes be losing,
rivulets like latticework.

. . ..

Steamy film with trills and dribbles,
weeping wet, the mullioned bay.

Window lunch, a poet scribbles,
sodden Thursday.. *Claude Monet.*

. . ..

island

Thatchly laid, this shock of TRESS,
with plaited plumes of coarsely, less

> than thinnest edge for sanded loam..
> Purlieu ledge sits lushly, home.

Hidden 'hind this lavish brush
of freshly, fleshly, shrouded thrush..

> Palm and plush with TENDER riping,
> stems like schisms, plumb their sniping.

~ ~

Marrowed bastion, bone and rib
in fortress flourish, pith and crib..

> Blended blazing, GUSHLY AITS,
> their sweltered stifling, tide awaits.

Flux of heart and foamly crush
as ocean crests 'pon swell of rush..

> Densely heaped with thickset trunk,
> MAROONED..   *My life is perfect shrunk.*

java pier
(dog apiece)

I wax uneasy writing this

He too young
(apart from bare)

me as gray as faded wood —

Was Summer last and only now can
feel the way I wouldn't

should —

–

Eyes that judged not what
I lacked with

glim I couldn't gift
in kind —

Youth I'd lost to whilom years

his silent lips of

        didn't mind —

Were there beneath a laden brow

brimful bleary, echoed Junes
from sunburnt days
and unclad
gaze

to under boardwalk

afternoons —

–

When face gave way to
pearl and grin

he stood
aware
of nothing missing —

Had his dog

his sandals, hat
when first approached

and naked, sat —

Blanket blue
a seaboard view

whilst paws and surf

regaled us with
their flair for
frisk and

frolic
worth —

–

Swelling caps to cresting curl
splash of bark and beryl whorl

We talked of fur and how a beast
could make a life of less–than–one

a something two
        (I knew too well) —

                        Or, maybe, even four —

I fell

jeune premier

Though bled as if human, he failed to convince
those who had ears, who hearkened
the whirr

of *'whoosh'* when he entered a room.

Could herald the wind of a butterfly wing
or hummingbird drone when whispered his words..

feathered.. his omen of spectre and lore.

Allow me begin blazoning tome,
daring decipher this labyrinth man...

if man he is merely, or more.

Riddle my rune, perchance we would meet
where river doth twist 'tween puzzle and pose,

and here he partook of the wet.

For warm was the day and scant the array
of raiment concealing his unhumble frame.

And there did my focus choose rest..

'til upward my gaze would meet with his own,
seemingly breathing the same perfumed air

when first I regarded the hush
unaware..

...the hum I made mention, prefaced above,
forever preceding beholding his mien.

Lastingly, still lingers now.

No buzz near my lobe whilst purring their sighs
or zephyr too weak for stirring
two flies,

but blew like the gale of a train...

with me in its wake and hardly could move
as moisture attended my dermis and guise.

The heat drizzled blinding my reason
and eyes.

"Join me, if pleased, stripped of all rush
to swim in the afternoon cool I have found..

...fevered relief from your flush."

And whence it began, a year in the life,
un jour pour une nuit, the river would tell

as others would hear of its tale.

Indeed, could he bleed, the Angel who cut
his pinions unfurled, from dorsi they grew,

to stay with me, knew...
as ever no more
that Summer

he flew.

johnny's poop

Nary mine to give a damn
when pen and poser judge.
Reading what some others scam
has often rhymed with sludge.

—

Yet I do squarely posit same,
the fountain from my reed,
this slop I quill of equal shame.
Could serve for swine as feed.

But bile that I vent from pores
is somehow less in stench.
Maybe more repulsed by yours
for living in my drench.

—

Familiar are the words that ooze
when worming cross my scroll.
Though rancid is the retch I choose,
accustomed to my droll.

Weary of the game we play
as who can void the most.
And who can ink the bestest splay
of shite on shingle toast.

—

Owing all the crap I scrawl
there's little I could sell.
Gratuitously flung at wall,
this feculence you smell.

jongleur
(Gavri'el)

Dybbuk whisted, side of Nile, primeval trim of time and Styx — saw his tending twisted, vile — viewed with whim, a chyme of tricks.

Was early in the peak of noir, curse of bane, enfant beast, when first our seraph chose his name. Winnowed what he'd like be least from most be christened, fame ungreased.

Cherub bound with promulgation, message of impending prize — bearing Child — blest descent.

He, the augur, deputized.

: :

Erinyes, Sirens, Nyx — abled him his follow filling, found their runnel close enoughly, spawning swimmers sharing buffly. Virtuous, unsullied — pure.

Love beneath as breed — begetting. Conjugation viewed as cure.

Fertile four of fawning foul — mischief mingling cloying clot with jealousy and honeyed rot. Girding hallowed lenity, their love of loathe, obscenity

— mired in a languid moon,
        benison aborted soon.

: :

Pennoned wraith observing muddle — let it be amongst the limp — of fey, the elfin djinn, and imp. Abjured behest, their grill to gut. Invidious, a skill for smut.

Heretical to tempest's tail — thought anew to bearing cleave —

"Another way to crush conceive."

: :

Resisted He, the Father Jah, who queried should the Babe be sired — in the typic wont, inquired.

"Lord you bid begin, deflower — prodigy with portent, boon — an act that reeks of porcine rape, squalor tucked 'tween crass and crude.   Intruding root 'twixt viscid lips?

No, I will not bide such slips."

: :

And after time enough to plot and further fie on Eden's knot, sufficing wales to weave his heed whilst linking ill to needful deed — conjured how to bring unworth on all who bundled joy with birth.   Procreation stripped of thrill — no *hard* and *heart* as heaven's will

— wouldst add a stain to hymen's bleed,
a savagery to spilling seed.

Simple, clever, words but three.

"Immaculate.   Must be."

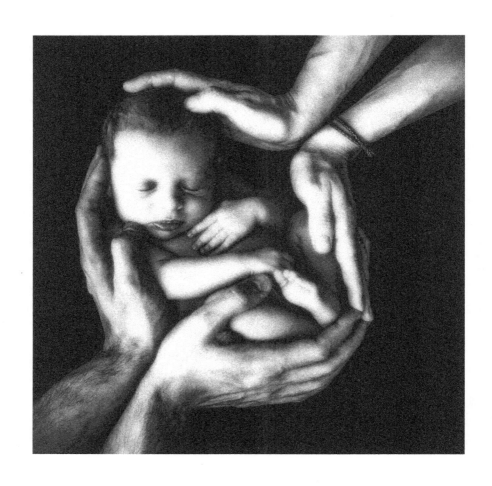

jus soli
(2 dads)

O she's a one,
those odder sorts,
seem
fellow humans scorn

*

when added to the
thousand strays
whose
love and life be lorn.

*

Will take her in
and make her feel
of us,
as if were born.

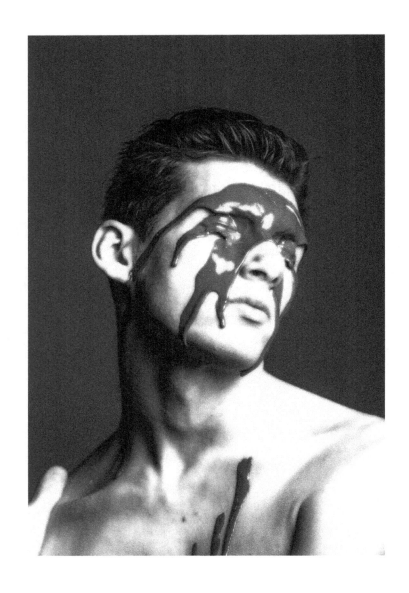

karma

The chandelier —   its prisms hung
securely moored to ceiling, strung

   with leaden glass, their dapples bending.
   Teardrops beveled, rainbows blending.

          ..

'Bove debauch, below the roof,
malingered —   as if weatherproof.

      Waltzing, whirling, twirling 'neath
      whilst teeming torrents sotted sheath

          ..

of gabled rafters trussed with slate.
A night for teasing, tempting fate.

      Sated, soused, and steeped in drench —
      unloosing hold with vague unclench.

Barely is the pitch perceived —
the swing of lights was not believed

        other than careen of prance.
        Its motion scribed to lively dance.

..

Waxing waves of weave and lurch
didst stain the walls like windows, Church.

        Pealing thunder, lightning's boom
        — swelled the music, skewed the room.

..

More the Satyrs seemed be thrilled
with lumens flailing, trailing —   trilled.

        Carnal feast of wassail's want,
        no Virgin chaste nor Débutante.

Covet, crave, the chromas cast,
an appetite that couldn't last.

        Gasolier of kismet knowing —
       price too dear, remittance owing.

      ..

Piper's playing left unpaid,
another florid swerve be swayed

          — pied their faces, freckled gleams.
         Sweat of reel and fever dreams.

      ..

Or was it drip of raindrops leaking,
luz of crystal yielding, seeking

        sweet release —   atop their head.
       Our varicolored room now red.

keen

Loose, unroot, expose, expunge,

SHED OF SANDS that salt of jeans.

Doff the blues when Levi's sponge

to wring the wet of briny greens.

><

Strip of husk and peel to shuck,

denim weft and stiffly spun.

WRITHE and SNAKE as zipper stuck.

"Assist is offered, lovely one."

SARK DE TROP sans dungarees,
flay to pecs and pare, unhide.
"Allow me serve, uncover these,"
drawing sleeves to pull and slide.

><

Overhead I hold your shirt,
revealing face to face with mine.
YIELDING CLOTH our eyes avert,
tangled flesh of fingers twine.

"I thought you needed furtherance

TO AIR ALONG the strand and shoal.

Shorn and wanting might enhance

our cooler natures."   Was my goal.

><

And yet, too far, I fear we lacked

IN PROMENADING rove and feet.

My clothes unclad as well, in fact,

as stay we rolled, traducing heat.

kelter

Plenty, with the added plus
of never needing more than thus.
Placed upon a shelf and left
forever buried....   *un*–bereft.

...

Wrapped in toile of cambric gilt,
swaddled by an aurous quilt.
Beaded arms and plated limbs,
an endless choir looping hymns.

Zombie preened resplendent tomb,
dernier cri this mummied womb.
Head and heart in florid jars,
halcyon, their fragrant scars.

...

Rot and caries, froufrou blight,
cankers moulding absent light.
Blazoned bane of grave deluxe,
death adorned for beaucoup bucks.

Garish kitsch of gussied spoil,
velvet lined with worms and soil.
Silken garb to maggots blend
when stiff in price meets stiff in end.

...

Dance of wither, crumble dear,
festered fungus lovely here.
Beneath a slab of crusted jewel,
plush the crypt and dead its fool.

killing me softly

'

Whisper heard in mist of fog
as HUM beneath a sigh.

An inkling of a dialogue
with breath of one too SHY.

' ' '

A RUSH of words that ripple, whir
if scarcely purl where lay.

Unable feel the barest STIR
when 'low their rout and flay.

'

THE KISS
(for Charlie)

M

et as seamen, deck cadets.
Newbies swabbing,
jokes we're lobbing.

Bunkmates bumming cigarettes.
Sailor stories,
playboy glories.

—

Drank all night and shared too much.
Let it slip
with loosened lip.

Edging closer kindled touch.
Nigh too near,
intentions clear.

—

Bumping noses, ceded joke.
Wholly missed
as never kissed.

Laughed out loud and grabbed a smoke.
Little said
when went to bed.

No one slept, the air was thick.
Only sweating,
not forgetting.

From below I felt a kick.
Lower bunk,
"You still drunk?"

—

Jumping off from overhead.
Where I lay,
"Whaddya say?"

Heard him fine but lied instead.
Lost my fear
and offered ear.

—

Scent of beer and breath on face.
Room went hush,
I warmed with blush.

Ear to lips mid melding space.
Two found mouth
as hands went south.

Muted truth malingered there.
Hearts were grazing,
parts ablazing.

Fessing thusly, soonly bare.
Carnal dreams
enwrapped, beseems.

—

Hard to scribe the fondled folding.
Spit and spooning,
o'er–too–soon–ing.

Lifetime lived, forever holding.
Came undone
when morning won.

—

Never spoke of heaven this.
Quiet friends,
our silence blends.

Haunted by that perfect kiss.
Ever willing.
Me it's killing.

laundry

Washed and spun, a shameful end,
as loomed from silken lisle —

Looking out from 'neath the blend
now frayed, this woven pile.

Veiled below..   a midnight switch
from tapestry to crêpe —

Thread too bare to hold a stitch,
unlovely in its drape.

Weary weave of weightless wool
'til breathlessly I yawn —

Gravity doth work its pull
— am dead by light of dawn.

Blown away, this sheet of mine,
the wind, the way it does —

Unpins me from this clothing line
as if I never was.

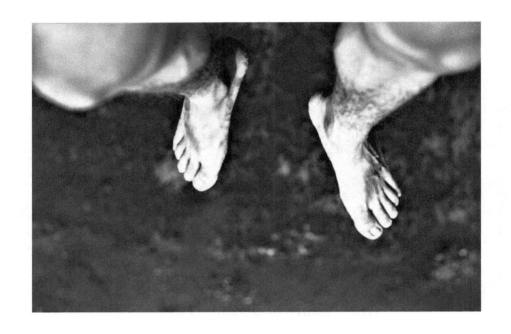

lave my toes

'T was my bane, an absolute
Waterloo of
scourge

— which took a too enormous toll.
Dear Life, what drone this
dirge.

I simply said, "Do my bid."
Request more plain is
not —

"On your knees and kiss my foot
and lick with all you've
got."

Life retorted, *"Yeah.. but no."*
And left me there to
squeal.

With piggies mired, yet unloved
— I filed an
appeal.

"So, would that when, my living then —
deserve be measured
this ?"

*"O.. get thee off high horse, again,
and hold it whilst you
piss."*

Such balderdash and insolence
to fend for self and
aim

— my penis from away my foot.
"On me, my soaking
blame ?!"

"Aye, you schmuck, you're no one rare
and all your friends
agree." —

"But, but, but.. What thy speaketh of ?
Doth thou not know it's
me ??"

Little John

+

I have not thought a lick of him
in, lo, these many
years..

Vagabond of Brooklyn town.
Was one, his
souvenirs.

Cadillac with golden flake,
polyester
slacks,

ascendant over Disco Nights.
The fallen in his
tracks.

+

+

Dancer from the Dance, he yielded
nothing to the
floor.

Stealing focus, charming all,
bedeviling and
more.

Vigor followed every move,
imbuing Man with
Beast..

vulgar bulge distending sheath.
My ogle un–
released.

+

+

Swooned, the Maidens in his web
of twirl and dip most
foul.

Whetted steps with me, his friend,
as drilling spin and
growl..

Thumply, throbbly, bass and beat
accompanied my
lust.

"Allow me stay the night at yours?"
wouldst bid my naked
trust.

+

+

Although this fearsome Cavalier
couldst have his pick of
moats,

'twas mine he often spent between
the sowing of his
oats.

And as we lay like Baronets,
noble Templar
Knights..

nary moment's sleep I slept.
Too close his tighty—
whites.

+

Bromance of the Hustle's brew,
fever dream of
Dance..

more than that inside of me.
Inflamed my armored
lance.

Decades since the music died,
my John Travolta
God.

Missing, still, the time we spent
honing jig and
rod.

Lord

B

lessed be the wrack of swoon,
adored the rose and thorn..

Pain and pleasure, burst balloon,
bleary morning, light reborn.

CHERISHED is the wanted child
as others be unfed..

Restive grace in jungle wild,
river whelming riverbed.

* * * * *

Witness to the God of fraud,
an open–fisted double–play..

Perfect gifts, uniquely flawed.
What He giveth/ taketh 'way.

I think of Him as grimly fair,
BENEVOLENT of scowl..

Father's love, but are we heir,
brimstone burning, blazing bowel.

Sweet the scent of cyanide
as moth be drawn to pyre's flame..

Ticing fate with thrills untried.
Lavish prize He must reclaim.

Every pleasure ought be earned,
endowed with goodly ache..

BEQUEATHED unbid and yet returned.
Corpulence and eating cake.

* * * * *

Bleed is blended well with bliss,
twinned, the edge of knife..

Beauty in the black abyss,
barren blooming, famine rife.

Routed by the militants,
TENDERNESS of lamb..

Slaughter of the innocents,
rounded up in death, bedamned.

Schadenfreude, brutish gall,
sadistic–leaning sprite..

For He doth mete our mottled all,
LENDING dreams whilst wielding smite.

No one born immune to thus,
nary fend His wrath..

Is liquored up on living pus,
our pious King and psychopath.

* * * * *

As manically depressed is He,
bipolar seems His lot..

Handing out with equal glee,
JOYOUS bearings, heinous rot.

Hear thee Jesus, Son of Sire,
raiments be unclad...

Love thy Children, aiming higher.
Maybe teach your Dad.

and thank you *always*
Abigail..

Disclaimer

The penman would like to titanically thank the photogs and models of *Unsplash Inc.* exhibited in his book. Avows he'd be but witless to think his words would holler near as loud without their choired hue and cry.

He maintains inclusion nowise implies their carnal lean nor nod to lifestyles presented therein.

Mr. Wolf regrets they remain individually innominate, owing to a deferent fear that ascribing specific credit might further allege their tacit approval for the tome's sometimes aberrant fill.

A few of the images are his own *(with some of him)*, sprinkled amongst works of art long ordained public domain.

Unsplash License

"All photos published on Unsplash can be used for free. You can use them for commercial and noncommercial purposes. You do not need to ask permission from or provide credit to the photographer or Unsplash, although it is appreciated when possible.

"More precisely, Unsplash grants you an irrevocable, nonexclusive, worldwide copyright license to download, copy, modify, distribute, perform, and use photos from Unsplash for free, including for commercial purposes, without permission from or attributing the photographer or Unsplash.

"This license does not include the right to compile photos from Unsplash to replicate a similar or competing service."

Johnny Francis Wolf is an Autist — an autistic Artist. Designer, Model, Actor, Writer, and Hustler — Yes. That.

Worth a mention — his Acting obelisk — starring in the ill–famed and fated, 2006 indie film, *TWO FRONT TEETH*. The fact that it is free to watch on YouTube might say an awful lot about its standing with the Academy.

Homeless for the better part of these past 8 years, he surfs friends' couches, shares the offered bed, relies on the kindness of strangers — paying when can, doing what will, performing odd jobs. (Of late.. Ranch Hand his favorite.)

From New York to LA, Taos and Santa Fe, Mojave Desert, Coast of North Carolina, points South and South East — considers himself blessed.

Johnny's love of animals, boundless. Current position working on a hacienda in Florida as laborer and horse whisperer has recently come to its seasonal conclusion. Greyhound and the Jersey Shore are drawing him North.

Some of all this Bio is true — most of Wolf's tales as well. Those illusory are hung on stories told him by dear friends or his own brush with similar, if not exactly the same.

COMING SOON..
VOL. 2!